Kool-Aid Ain't So Bad

Richard T. Biviano

authorHOUSE®

AuthorHouse™
1663 Liberty Drive
Bloomington, IN 47403
www.authorhouse.com
Phone: 1-800-839-8640

First published by AuthorHouse   5/18/2011

ISBN: 978-1-4343-0908-2 (sc)

Library of Congress Control Number: 2007902723

Printed in the United States of America

<u>DEDICATE</u>

I dedicate this journal to my children and their
children in the hope that one day one of them will continue
to pass on our history to the next generation.

CONTENTS

Introduction

On January 28, 2004 an event occurred that would not only change my life, but my feelings towards my own mortality. First, I become a member of a fast growing fraternity called the "Zipper Club," and I am not a person who joins clubs. If I had been given the choice to join one I would have joined the volunteer fire department instead. Lying in a hospital bed for eight days gave me plenty of time to think about how truly lucky I had been to this point in my life. You're so busy in your early years that you don't take the time to totally enjoy and savor life as it is, I know I didn't. I've had time now to remember the growing up of not only my family, but myself as well. I have memories of things like rice pudding, white shoes, Amish water, and the screwball songs I taught my children. I'll explain all of this later. While lying in my hospital bed my thoughts went to a particular time or event in my life. I smiled and even laughed out loud once, prompting the patient who shared the room with me to ask, "What's so funny, I thought you were in a lot of pain." What he didn't know, of course was, I was reliving a conversation I had with my son Daniel when he was seven years old about rice pudding. When I told him the story, he laughed out loud and we started talking about our families. The two of us lay in our beds until the wee hours of the morning telling each other our life's story. His was a little sad because he was brought up by his aunt, and not his parents. Since he was the oldest child, he along with his aunt raised his two younger sisters. He was an unforgettable character, and I mean the "character" in its broadest form. After telling some stories about my children, he said he hadn't laughed that much in years and told me I should put the stories in a notebook so everyone could enjoy them. I told him I wasn't interested in writing a notebook. All I wanted to do was get out of this hospital and go home and start living again. After going home I started twelve weeks of rehab for my heart. After a few weeks I met him again, and he asked if I jotted down the stories. I told him I had forgotten about it. After he left I started thinking about what he had said, and I thought to only write about the funny things my children did would not be much of a story. The story has to be about me and how I grew up, with the good things that happened as well as the not so good. This has to be about my memories which will of course include my children. My Mother had passed away the year before my surgery as did the only aunt that I had left on my father's side. I was now left with no living blood aunts or uncles on either side of the family. With no ties to the passed I started to realize how little I knew about my family until I tried to get information about them. There's no one left to pass on the history of the family to my two sons and daughter, as well as my grandchildren. The more I thought about the story, the more the flashbacks and memories came. I was unable to connect the dots between my memories and the flashbacks, so I jotted them down anyway, just for the record. Had any of the close relatives been alive, I would have had the luxury of their input and cleared up the fuzziness I have about my early childhood. But I don't, so here we are.

My own family has had its ups and downs along with smiles and frowns but we always seemed to bounce back on our feet. Even thought we didn't have much money in those early days, the images of the time were saved on photos taken with my 127 instamatic camera and an old box camera. I have sixteen three inch ring photo albums full of pictures that were taken over the years of the family. Every time I open one of these albums to add more pictures, I get to enjoy the memories again. Over the years my wife and I, and particularly my children, have on many occasions opened these albums to take a peek into the past. We have all relived these times and have said, do you remember when. These albums as well as some old 8mm films, videos, my high school year book and a box full of souvenirs along with my own memories prompted me to begin this journal.

Life is a time when good things and bad things happen, it matter not if you are rich or poor you still have the memories. I don't what to dwell on the negative things that happened, but they did happen and they are memories. What I want is to hang on tight to the positives, because this makes the good even better. I thought everyone had it better than me when I was young, but as I look in retrospect I guess I didn't have it so bad after all. We have hundreds of happy and enjoyable moments that will stay with us forever. There are as many unpleasant ones as well, but we try to push these to the back of the line. I don't think my life was any different than yours was, we all have a story to tell, because it is our legacy.

Everything you read here is about my life as I remember it. After saying all of the above, it's time for me to share these memories and experiences with you. One thing I want to mention is the lack of the last names of people mentioned in my story. I did this for a reason I didn't forget them, just didn't want to embarrass or make anyone feel uncomfortable. It's now January 2010 and a long time since I put my first words down. To the readers who are members of the "Zipper Club" I hope my journey makes you smile a little and think back to those great moments and events you had prior to your surgery. To those who are not members of this club, I do not recommend joining unless it is absolutely necessary or you have nothing else better to do. Either way, the story starts now.

CHAPTER 1
NORWICH & THE BEGINNING

The tale begins in Norwich, a small town in upstate New York and the county seat of Chenango County. It may not sound like much, but it was where I was born. The town itself is old, and getting older. The first house was built in 1790, and by 1816 it had enough of a population to be called a town. The town grew fast, and in 1914 with a population of over ten thousand, it officially became a city by charter. The city limits extend from the Chenango River on the east to the Canasawacta Creek on the west. Incase you wish to know, Chenango is an Indian name for the flower called bull thistle, which you can find all over the County. Besides being the county seat, it was also the cultural center of the county. The one real big landmark in the city was the old Eagle Hotel built in the 1800's and located on Broad Street, which today is route 12. Norwich was the half way mark for the stagecoach coming to and from Syracuse or Utica to Binghamton. The stage would stop over night in Norwich and the passengers would spend the night in the Eagle Hotel. During its hay day some very important people stayed there, among the notables were Teddy Roosevelt, Buffalo Bill Cody, and P. T. Barnum. Robert E. Lee was also reported to having stayed in Norwich around 1860. Not only did Norwich have a colorful history with notable characters staying there, but it was also the beginning of my life

I was born in Norwich on January 29, 1933 under the sign of Aquarius. I was told many years later that I weighted six pounds and fourteen ounces at birth. My Mothers name was Angelina, but everyone called her Jean. She was born in Atlantic City, New Jersey on Christmas day December 25, 1909, the second oldest of five sisters and one brother. It's interesting when you come from a small town, how or why your parents came to live in Norwich in the first place. The only thing I can think of is, you're either born there or you migrated there for a reason, such was why my Mother ended up in

Norwich. Her oldest sister Vera met and married my uncle Wendell, who was in the Coast Guard stationed in Atlantic City at the time. After his leaving the Coast Guard, they moved to Norwich, his home town, where they finally settled down. My mother had left school when she finished the eighth grade to help support the family. Work was scarce at that time in Atlantic City and my mother needed to work, so in 1927 she moved in with my Aunt Vera, found work at the Norwich Knitting Company where she met and later married my father on October 28, 1929. Another of my mothers' sisters, Rose, came to Norwich later and also found work at the Knitting Mill. She also met, married and settled down there. This is how and why my mother settled in Norwich. .My Grandmother, on my mothers side, came from the Naples area in Italy around 1900. I really didn't know much about my grandparents because we lived so very far from them and I can't remember the subject ever coming up. The only memories I have of them as a youngster were the times we visited them during the war years, and I'll cover that later. My father's name was Pasquale, but everyone called him Pat or Patsy. He was born in Norwich on September 22, 1907. He, like my mother, also had to leave school after the ninth grade to help support his family. He was the second oldest of nine children, five sisters and three brothers. His parents came from the village of Salemi, near the seaport of Masala on the Island of Sicily.

I have very few memories of my life prior to age seven or eight. This could be because I'm getting older and finally losing it or maybe because I've just plain forgotten, but either way most of my early years are only flashbacks and occasional thoughts that are sketchy at best. But they were my memories and flashbacks so I wrote them down anyway.

I still remember my grandparents and their home on Railroad Street. They lived in a brick house directly across the street from the O&W (Ontario and Western Railroad Station) where my grandfather worked as a fireman and a stoker on a steam engine. I was their first grandson, as in most of the older Italian homes of that time, I was king.I'm not sure what I was the king of, but I held the title. I have fleeting memories of birthday cakes baked by my Grandmother and the big fuss my aunts made over me. I remember my Grandmother was always squeezing my face between her hands and kissing me and rattling off something in Italian. We never spoke Italian in our house and I've often regretted the fact that I never really learned how to understand and speak the language. I don't remember living in a second story apartment next to my grandparents, but my Mother or Father had mentioned it from time to time as I was growing up. On the opposite side of my grandparents house was the Ontario Hose Company, a volunteer fire company with one fire truck, and next to them the Norwich Knitting Mill warehouse. I remember Railroad Street being a dirt road until it was paved many, many years later. I can vaguely remember eating oatmeal and cream of wheat twice a day during the Depression. I was told my father was only working one or two days a week at that time. The Depression may have been over when I was born, but times were still tough late into the 1930s. When I was about five or six years old we moved from the apartment next door to my Grandparents to a house on Birdsall Street. I remember the house being a lot bigger and definitely a lot quieter. I remember having a huge back yard that my Father turned into a garden where he grew just about every vegetable that we ate. The only other thing I remember about the house was the address and the school was only four blocks away.

In 1941 my parents bought our house on Griffin Street, which was located three properties down from the Knitting Mill where they both worked, and a five minute walk to my Grandparents house on Railroad Street. This house needed a lot of work but my father was handy with tools and little by little he got it into shape. I was to have my own room and my sister Pat had hers. Our house was in the middle of the block. On one side of our property were houses, but on the other was a greenhouse, which adjoined our driveway and next to that a vacant house, and then the Norwich Knitting Mill. The greenhouse, which was located between the vacant house and our house, had a side entrance that was just off of our driveway. The old man who worked there would use the driveway entrance to get to and from work every day and I became friends with him. He used to let me in the greenhouse to watch him pot flowers on this long wooden bench. The first thing I noticed when I walked in was the smell of fertilizer mixed with damp soil in a sun filled glass room that was filled with flowers. It's a smell you can get nowhere else but in a greenhouse. Whenever I walk into a florist today I get that same aroma and sometimes I think back to those days.

While writing down the experience in the greenhouse, I remembered something else that stuck in my memory. It was something that seldom, if ever is heard today, it's the sound of coal running down a coal shoot into your basement. The coal man would back his truck into our driveway, line up the coal shoot with the cellar window, open a sliding door on the truck and let the coal run. The sound of the coal coming out of the truck and onto a coal shoot running into the coal bin in our cellar was deafening, but alluring to an eight year old boy. After the coal is dumped, the shoot shines like a brand new nickel, but if you run hands over it, they turn jet black from the soot. Remember, you're looking and hearing this through the eyes and ears of an eight year old boy. One of my chores was to take the ashes from the furnace out of the cellar and dumping them in our garden, where my father would mix it with the garden soil. I would have to sift it through a wire screen first to reclaim the coals that were mixed in with the ashes. I usually got about a bucket full of coal every time. For your information, there are two kinds of coal that were used in your furnace, chestnut coal for the fire and pea coal for the fire bed at night. I remember my mother taking my sister Pat and I to the Endicott-Johnson Shoe store to buy shoes. She called them Easter shoes, but in reality they were for school and for dress. This was the only time during the year we got new shoes. When we were being fitted for shoes, you would walk over to this contraption, it was actually an X-ray machine, to see if the shoes fit properly. It was neat looking through a scope to see if your feet and the bones inside of your new shoes fit properly. If the old shoes still fit but had holes in the soles, we would take them to a shoemaker and have them half-soled, or if the heels were worn down they were replaced. If they were still usable, and fit us after we got the new ones, we wore them for play. I don't want you to think we were the only one who did this, because everyone else was pretty much in the same boat. Remember this was the middle 30s and money was tight.

Christmas was always spent at my Grandparents house. The week before Christmas, my father and his brothers bought fresh pork, which they ground up, mixed in some seasoning, pushed it into some pig casings and tied them into links. It made the greatest sausages I've ever tasted. This was what my Grandmother used to make the sauce for the pasta dishes we had at the Christmas dinner. Christmas morning was always spent at my Grandparents house. After the morning mass everyone would meet at their house for fried sausage, peppers and onions on hot fresh Italian rolls. What a treat that was, I can still smell the cooking sausage. This tradition pretty much stayed the same until she passed away.

I remember my grandfather taking me down to the railroad yard to see the roundhouse where he worked. I'll never forget the sight of a big steam engine on this giant turntable being moved around to a stall where it was to have work done on it. I even got the chance to climb aboard an engine that had stopped on a side rail. What a thrill that was. I have another clear memory of him taking me there when a steam engine with black smoke bellowing out of the smoke stack as it passed us by. The smoke was full of small sparks of burning wood falling on my cloths, burning tiny holes in my shirt. When he brought me home and my Mother saw the tiny holes, boy was she very angry at him. All of the O&W railroad tracks and buildings are gone now. Where the round house was, is the approximate location of the new centralized High School, new apartments and houses. Today, nothing relating to the O&W is there anymore.

I had spent a few days with friends in Norwich a while back and decided one day to look around town. I was shocked at what I saw. The house my Grandparents lived in has disappeared, there is no evidence of it ever existing or of the family that once lived there, but I know, and I'll never forget it. The employees of the company that bought that piece of the property use it to eat their lunch there or park their cars. I don't know which. The Knitting Mill, which was directly across the street from their home, has been demolished. There are new buildings there now, but the properties next to them are still there. I remember them as a Bakery, a Bar and Grille and an Italian Grocery Store. Right now, they are just run down empty skeletons of the pass. Around the corner from there was where I grew up. I was again shocked to see most of the old neighborhood in dire need of repair and paint, including my own.

Looking at Norwich through the eyes of an adult today, I see a picturesque town set in the middle of the Chenango valley with rolling hills on either side of its city limits. I see colorful fall scenes, and snow covered hills in the winter. I still remember the cool summer nights, the county fair every August, along with the sulky races where I used to make a couple of dollars cleaning out the stables. I remember the clambakes at the fair grounds, and the summer "Lucky Teeter and his Hell Drivers" came to town and put on a daredevil car act.

Norwich had the Knitting Mill, the Pharmacy, and a large supermarket warehouse center, along with a hammer and tool factory, a toilet seat factory and what I thought was a thriving business and shopping area along Broad Street. We had two movies theaters, the Colonia, which is still there and Smalley's where the Saturday matinees showed Roy Rogers, Gene Autry and Hopalong Cassidy westerns along with a serial following the movies. I still remember the Green Hornet, Buck Rogers, and Flash Gordon, how each chapter ended, and how they would get out of whatever dilemma they might have been in the chapter before. After the movie was over, if I had a nickel left, I bought an ice cream cup. After removing the cover, you peeled off the protected wax paper and had a round picture of a cowboy on the inside of the cover. Just up the street from Smalley was the DL&W (Delaware, Lackawanna & Western) Depot. The train no longer runs now, but the Depot is still there and occupied by the town as the Norwich Municipal Building. Across the street from the Depot is a real old landmark. An old railroad caboose painted red and converted to a small eatery known as Benny's Diner. I remember passing that diner every day on my way to and from school. I've even had coffee and a donut there on a few occasions with friends of mine in the early days. This diner has got to be at least seventy years old and if I remember correctly its' still open for business today. There was a YMCA and of course the Chenango Memorial Hospital, where I spent some time. I'll talk about that later. We even had a semi-pro baseball and football team called the Norwich Blue Jays.

There were two parks at the main red light where North and South Broad streets crossed East and West Main Streets. This was the center for most of the town events.

Band concerts were held on the gazebo in the park on East Main Street every Friday night, weather permitting. I've been told this tradition is still going strong today and I'm glad to hear that. Every Saturday morning the park was surrounded by a farmers market. This was a typical small town where people lead a simple life. This market is one of the few things that has never changed. There are four places in town where I spent a great deal of time during my junior and senior years in high school, the Bluebird Cafe, Garff's Soda Fountain & Cigar Store, and the two Parks. I also spent a lot of time at Chenango Lake for picnics and swimming. We even had a drive in theater just outside of town that showed movies on Friday and Saturday nights. Even though I didn't realize it at the time, it was truly a great place to grow up. People seemed to be generally happy and working, but like me, Father Time has caught up with us. The town and I have changed a lot since those days. The Eagle Hotel was gone when I came home from the Navy, Garff's was still there, but not the hangout it once was, now its a deli.. The Bluebird is gone and replaced by a pizza parlor, just what the world needs, another pizza parlor. The parks are still there but have taken on a modern look. The old wooden gazebo has been replaced by one made of brick that has no real character. The Canasawacta Creek was dammed up to form the Norwich Swimming Pool where everyone went for a summertime swim or just a place to hang out. This has been replaced by this huge hole in the ground, lined with concrete, painted green and filled with chlorinated water. I'm not saying this is bad, just different. This was also where the High School held its track and field meets. The field has been replace by a parking area for the pool and moved to the location of the new high school, where the old roundhouse used to be. I think if all the places that I've mentioned could talk, every teenager of that time, would be a little nervous today.

The population of the town has since gone down and most of the industry has departed for parts unknown. The Norwich Knitting Company was the largest employer of people in town at that time has moved south. This was the company where my Mother and Farther worked for the better part of their lives. The greenhouse that was next to my house is no longer there, and neither is the "Haunted House" where we tried out the home make firecrackers. These have been replaced with a fenced in paved parking lot that was used for a while by the Knitting Mill. The last time I had gone by the old house was after my Mother passed away, and the lot and the Mill were vacant. The buildings were there, but they looked like ghosts of the past. The Ontario Hotel, at the end Griffin Street is there, but everything else from there to East Main Street are gone. At one time there was a bakery next to the Mill, after that a bar and grille, and then the corner grocery store. All of these are missing today, even the barber shop where I got my hair cut. The one big thing I still remember about the barber shop was this big reproduction hanging on the back wall of "Custer's Last Stand." This painting had to be at least three feet wide and five feet long. At least that was how I remembered it. The Norwich Pharmaceutical Co, which carried the town name on its products, primarily a burn cream called, Unguantine, all over the world has merged with another company and left town. The old Borden Condensed Milk buildings, which were vacated when they left, were taken over by the Victory Chain Stores for a warehouse that stocked food for all of their stores in the state of New York. They were then taken over by another company, and then they left town. These companies and a few others were the backbone for the paychecks that the people earned and now there are no big employers. A few small companies have come to town, but they could never support the number of people who needed work. It's a shame that my town and so many other small towns across the country have fallen on hard times.

The general shopping is done mostly at the Wal-Mart store about four miles outside of town, while the food shopping is done on the outskirts of town next to the Cemetery and the Old Pettis Slope where we skied and tobogganed as youngsters. Broad Street today is nothing more than wide road going through the middle of old town. There are very few traces of the past as I remember them, my Grandfathers house, the O & W, the Bluebird, the swimming pool and all the rest, but like the passing of a family or an era its' going to happen. I only get back to town once every five years or so for the class reunions and an occasional visit with friends. It makes me sad to see the decline, and I'm sure there are many valid reasons for this. I know it was a simpler time then, with no boom-blasters, televisions, drugs, or fast living, but I still like to remember it as it was in my time, and I guess I always will.

1-1

Mon & Dad Wedding Picture

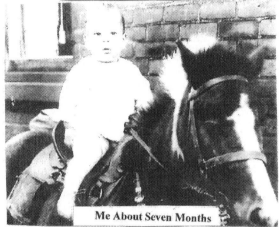

Me About Seven Months

Me About One Year Old

Grandfather – Grandmother
50th. Anniversary (Mom)

Mom, Sisters Rose & Margaret
Future Uncle Armand
Lake Lenape – 1939

1-2

Friend – My Father – Uncles Angelo and Tony – 1935

Aunt Helen 1940

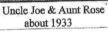

Uncle Joe & Aunt Rose
about 1933

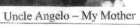

Uncle Angelo – My Mother

Uncle Nick 1939

Griffin Street – Now

Grandparents Old Location

9

3

Gone forever   Bakery   Bar & Grille   Grocery Store

Colonia Theater Now and Then

Garf's Soda Fountain - Now A Deli

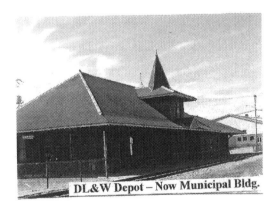

DL&W Depot – Now Municipal Bldg.

Benny's Diner

CHAPTER 2
THE WAR YEARS

I was eight years old when the Japanese bombed Pearl Harbor on December 7, 1941and the start of World War II. I had no idea where Pearl Harbor or the Hawaiian Islands were, I only knew what I heard from adults. Later when I heard Hitler and Germany declared war against us I'm not sure I knew who he was or where Germany was. I doubt very much that I even knew what a war was. The first time I had ever seen a picture of Hitler was a frontal facial cartoon of him in the funny papers. They had pictured him with black hair falling down over his forehead covering part of his right eye, and a small black mustache under his nose. The cartoon also showed Tojo, the Japanese leader, with a big round face wearing a pair of huge eyeglasses that covered his two slanted eyes. He also had three buck teeth and big ears. I may never have heard about these places or people, but it wasn't long before I learned want was going on. I have some very vivid memories for that period of time. Our house, on Griffin Street, put usabout a half block away from the O & W RR where we got to see what the enemy looked like. We would see German and Italian prisoner of war trains going north to the POW camps. Sometimes they would stop to get water for the steam engines, and I would run down to the depot to see the prisoners, only to find out they didn't look any different than us. We were never allowed to get near them, but we could look. I was really impressed with the army MPs who were dressed in uniforms and guarding the prisoners, while holding Tommy guns. Even though no one was allowed to get near them, I saw women from the Italian section on Norwich sending the Italian prisoners fruit, and converse with them in Italian about the "old country." The German prisoners were more of a sullen looking bunch, as compared to the Italians who were generally laughing. I think they liked it when so many people spoke to them in their own language. I guess they didn't realize they were passing through the Italian section of Norwich. There were other times when the trains were carrying Navy Seabees to the base at Sampson. I remember them hanging out of the windows of the train hooting and whistling when ever there were pretty girls around. I didn't understand why then, but I do now. When ever the train stopped for any length of time, they would be ordered out of the train, and marched up Griffin Street and do calisthenics right in front of my house. As the war progressed I became more and more interested in it. All everybody ever talked about was the war and who was being drafted or enlisted and who was where, and later who was killed, missing or wounded. The only source of information available was the radio or what they read in the paper, while those who had someone in the service would receive letters with some news in it. This in itself wasn't very much, because the letters were being censored by the military before they were delivered to the addressee. Years later we found out the government had kept a lot of information from us, primarily those that dealt with causalities, or where the fighting was going on if we were on the short end. Remember, there wasn't any television cameras or CNN reporters sitting on the battle field making videos for the six o'clock news.

Everybody was doing something to help the war effort, including school children. I remember taking scrap metal and aluminum to the Birdsall Street School and putting it into these huge enclosed pens on the lawn in front of the school. After the pen was filled there would be a truck coming by to pick it up. I never knew where it was going, but I thought it was being taken somewhere to make things for war. The schools were also selling war bonds and stamps. The stamps coast ten cents each and when you had $18.70 worth of stamps you traded them in for a twenty-five dollar war bond. Every once in a while my Mother would give me some change, and I would take my stamp book and the change to school for the stamps. At Christmas time the class would send Christmas cards and fill small brown cardboard boxes with hard candy and little things, like soap, tooth brushes, combs, pads and pencils. we would all sign the Christmas card that was inside the box, and then it was mailed. I remember listening to the teacher reading us a letter she had received from soldiers who had gotten one of our boxes. They also sent us a picture of themselves opening the box we had sent, and our teacher tacked the letter and the picture on our bulletin board.

Aunt Margaret came to stay with us during the war years to work at the Sintilla Company in Sidney, New York. They made magnetos for the airplanes used in WWII. At the time she was engaged to my future Uncle Armand who was from Philadelphia. He had been drafted into the army before the war started as a peace time draftee. The National Service Emergency Regulation of 1940 required everyone over the age of eighteen to register for the peacetime draft. If your number was called, you were then required to serve one year in the army for military training. Once the war broke out, he was on his way to Africa where he he fought and later captured at a place called Kasserine Pass. He was held prisoner by the Italians, and later the Germans for twenty-seven months. When the war ended, they married in a military wedding in Philadelphia. I was ten when she came to live with us and I must admit I have some fond memories of her. She was what you might call a "Heller," and I got to know her and her two friends Rita and Vivian, who were also fun people, along with my fathers' sister Annie. The four of them would work all day, go out half the night and then come home early in the morning dead to the world. The train station was only a half block away, which was a good thing because they were catching the train to Sidney by the skin of their teeth every morning. My Father would holler at her all the time for staying out so late, but she could care less, it went in one ear and out the other. She was twenty two, single and on her own, having a good time as long as it lasted. I can still picture her standing in from of a mirror in the bathroom, dressed in her bath robe with a cigarette dangling from her mouth while trying to comb her hair. All the while watching the clock and complaining there wasn't enough time and she was going to miss the train. Little did I know, that years later I would be staying with her and my uncle for about a year and a half while I was going to Temple University at night, and working in the day time. I doubt that I would ever forget her, she was a lot of fun and an easy person to remember.

In the 1940's we didn't have video games like Donkey Kong and Super Mario, nor did we have computers with electronic games. What we had were simple games played with marbles, called "Goosies to the Pot", "Closest to the Wall" and "Bunks and Spans." These were just a few names of the many variations that were played with marbles. We also had a very popular game called "War" that was played with war cards. You could buy flat packs of gum at the "5 and 10 Store" for a nickel, each pack would contain two 2 ½ x 3 ½ inch war cards, plus the gum. The cards would have pictures of an air force plane, a battle scene, a picture of a battleship, or anything else related to the war. One of the players would call "Odd or Even" then the cards are flipped into the air to see how they landed. If you had call "Even" and the two cards matched when they landed you win. But, if the card were not alike, odd you lose. The game could be played for the one card you both were flipping, or you might each put three cards in a kitty and winner takes all. The object is to win the war and the cards, like marbles there were many variations of the game. Besides being used in the game, they were also used for trading, if you were a collector. At one time I had a cigar box full of these, but somehow they disappeared when I left home. I sure wish I had them today, they would be a collectors prize. If you were collecting the war cards, you would probably be collecting military shoulder patches as well. These were harder to get than the cards because the only way you could get them is if you knew someone in the military. When ever you were able to get duplicates of a patch, you could trade it with someone who also might have a double of one you wanted. I was real lucky, my Uncle Nick who was in the 8th Air Force stationed in England and later in France, would send me one or two different patches whenever he wrote a letter to my mother. He would send pictures of himself standing next to some bomber or fighter, with bombs on small dollies. He always looked so cool in his flight jacket. He was also a great saxophone player and had a chance to play for Tommy Dorsey before the war. Sixteen years later his band would play at our wedding. Before he passed away in 2002, he gave me his 557th Bombardment Squadron book that showed the history of his group in Europe. He said I would probably appreciate this more than anyone else, and he was right. Several of my other uncles sent me invasion money as souvenirs and a few patches as well. I still have a box full of the money, which includes several thousand original German mark notes. I can still picture my Uncle Wendell walking down Griffin Street with a duffle bag slung over his shoulder after being in Europe for over two years. It was a thrill seeing him in his uniform with a chest full of ribbons. We also played other outdoor game like pick-up baseball, kick the can and mumble dee peg to name a few more. Indoors, we played board games like Monopoly, Chinese Checkers, 500 Rummy, pick-up sticks and tiddley winks. I doubt that no more then a handful of today's kids have ever heard of tiddley winks or pick-up sticks. When we were a little older we played penny poker and spin the bottle. I don't think the kids of today realize how much fun it was to play outdoors. I had other cousins who also served in the army during the war and all became my idols. I looked at them as Gods to be worshiped. I was always wishing I could be in the army, wearing a uniform with all kinds of medals on my chest. I was just a boy filled with this sense of pride and knew absolutely nothing about what war was like.

Norwich had a huge tote board in the park on the corner of North Broad Street and East Main Street listing all of the men from Norwich who were in the service. There were hundreds and hundreds of names on it including my uncles and cousins. I noticed that there were gold stars after some of the names. When told that they had been killed in action, I don't think I really grasped the seriousness of this until later. I didn't know how many gold stars were on there, but there were an awful lot of them. On Memorial Day the American Legion Post would have a ceremony and fire a six gun salute. The young boys, me included, would scramble to pick up the spent shells after the six gun salute.

Ration stamps were a big part of our lives during the war, and gas rationing was one of the biggest. You needed coupons for gas, without the coupon you couldn't buy it. My father's car, a 1937 Graham-Paige, had a sticker similar to the inspection stickers that are on the cars today. This sticker would show the priority you had, based on how your car was being used. If you drove to and from work your sticker color might have been green with a capital A in the center. Your color and priority letter would show how much gas you could buy each week or what ever the time period was. But, your ration stamp must match the sticker on your windshield in color and priority letter, or you couldn't buy gas. I would like to add here that the station attendant would clean your windshield, check your oil and make sure you had enough air in your tires. When was the last time you had this kind service at the pump? Today you're lucky if he pumps the gas for you. Ration stamps were needed in order to buy food, clothing and shoes as well as gas. My sister Pat and I used to mix Nucco, an oleo margarine that had a large orange blister in the package filled with orange colored dye. You had to snap the blister then mix it in with the oleo lard to make it look like butter. It didn't really taste like butter, but it sure looked like butter. Every once in a while my father would bring home with some salt butter that he had traded for, and we mixed it into the Nucco. Now you had something that actually looked and tasted like butter.

During the war, just about everybody had or shared in a victory garden. This was one of the many ways that people helped on the home front. A large portion of thefood that was raised by the farmers were canned by commercial companies and went directly to the armed forces. If you wanted to eat well, you had a garden. My father and two other men were privy to a large piece of ground on East Main Street where they grew just about everything that had seeds, be it corn, beans or tomatoes, you name it. I remember them drying out the seeds for the next year's planting. My sister Pat and I had the job of shucking and scraping the corn off the cobs, peas out of the pods and snipping beans so my Mother could put them in jars for cooking. They would be put into large containers filled with water and cooked, this was called "canning." After they were cooked, we stored them in our dirt floor cellar on shelving my father had made. My father would bring home a bushel of pears or Bing cherries, from one of the farms and these were also canned and stored in the cellar. We never lacked for something to eat, thanks to that victory garden. We were by no means the only people who did this, it was this or you went hungry. You have to remember we were at war and it took ration coupons or stamps to get food from a grocery store, if it were available. Another thing he used to bring home were sacks of wild mushrooms that he had picked in the woods when he went hunting. He would clean them, then my mother would put them in a pan along with a silver dollar while they were cooking. After they were done, if the silver dollar turned black this meant they were tainted and had to be thrown away. If the silver dollar wasn't black, it was ok to eat them. I didn't think much about it back then, but no one died so it must have worked. Today, I doubt very much if I would gamble on the silver dollar making my decision to eat something that might be poisoned. He even dug out dandelions that grew in an open field that cows graze on. After he scrubbed them clean my mother would make a green salad or she cooked them. I never really liked them in a salad, they were very bitter. I only ate them when they were cooked because I didn't have a choice. When my father wasn't around I used call to it rabbit food. At times when I'm cutting the lawn and I see a dandelion, I smile, shake my head and mow them down. In addition to the victory garden and the canning, we had rhubarb growing wild along the fence in our back yard. They had thick stalks with huge elephant ear shaped leaves on the ends. We would cut the ends off, peel the outside of the stalk and dip it into some sugar that we had taken from the kitchen. It tasted like a piece of bitter sweet candy, and as I wrote this down, my mouth started to water. My father and mother both worked full time in the knitting mill, making clothes for the army. Life at this time was not easy, it seemed as though all you did was work, but then again, there was a war going on. Rationing and the war changed our way of life, and also changed the lives of the people who fought the war. In 1943 the copper penny was minted in lead because the copper and the brass that went into making the penny was needed for the war effort.

When I was eleven, my Mother took me with her to Atlantic City to see my grand-parents. Today you can drive from Norwich to Atlantic City in about five hours, but not then. We went by bus in the morning from Norwich to Binghamton and boarded a train named the "Phoebe Snow" that took us to Philadelphia where we would board another train to Atlantic City. The trip lasted all night and into the wee hours of the next morning. When we finally got there, I couldn't wait to go to the beach that I had heard so much about. My cousin Bob, who was a year younger than me, and I were told not to go into the water because it was full of oil, but we went in anyway. A ship had been sunk off the coast of Atlantic City by a German submarine that night causing crude oil to mix with the water and the sand. This black oil, that was in the water and on the sand, stuck to your skin like glue. When we finally went home, after being in the water all morning, my mother had to literally scrub these blotches of oil off my skin. I didn't think that the crude oil smelled very good either. I remember being very excited to be walking the boardwalk for the first time. My Aunt Helen had taken my cousin and I to a movie at the Steel Pier and afterward we stopped at a penny arcade to play games. Later, as we walked along the boardwalk I started to notice servicemen in wheelchairs and beach chairs being pushed up and down the boardwalk by nurses. Some of these soldiers were missing legs and or arms. My aunt told me that these were men who were wounded in the war and were staying at the hotels on the boardwalk. The government had taken over many of the big hotels and converted them into hospitals, convalesce, and rehab centers. A lot of these converted hotels are no longer there, having since been knocked down and replaced by buildings associated with the casino industry. But I'll never forget the sight that I saw that day. The following year my Aunt Vera, who went to see the Miss America Pageant every year, took me with her to Atlantic City. This trip in particular stands out because the war had ended while we were there. When the word was out that it was over, people on the boardwalk went crazy. They were dancing, hugging, kissing and celebrating in every way they could think of. I remember walking back to my grandparents' house listening to people blowing horns in their car, ringing bells, yelling, screaming and crying. That was something nobody could ever forget, at least I never did. While I was in Atlantic City, my cousin and I used to sleep on cots in the garage because all the bedrooms in the house were full. I'm sure we had more fun in the garage then we would have had in the house, besides it was a lot cooler there than it was in the bedrooms where there was no air conditioning. We were having a great time in the two weeks I spent there, but it went by much too fast and I really didn't want to go home. In spite of the war, I found Atlantic City to be lots of fun in the summer time. Besides the boardwalk and the beach there was the Steel Pier, Hammons Pier, the penny arcades and salt water taffy. The old Lyric Theater on Atlantic Ave. used to show western movies followed by a serial and after the movie we would cross the avenue and get us a Cho-Cho bar to eat on the way home. This was the first and only time I had ever seen square traffic lights at an intersection instead of round ones. I also remember riding the trolley cars and thinking how neat it was when they crossed at the intersection and throw off sparks when the trolley wheel on the roof met the cross over of the electric wire on the wheel. The trolleys are gone now and replaced by buses. You can no longer see the sparks that a young boy thought were neat and I don't think those Cho-Cho bars are around anymore either. All I know is the two times that I was there during the war years were solidly etched into my memory.

My father had won a Graham-Paige touring car at the Colonial Theater in 1937. He had purchased chances on it and his number was called on the stage of the Colonial Theater between the double feature of the movies. He kept that car all through the war years without any undercoating to protecting it from the salt that was used on the roads during the winter months. As a result, it gradually rusted through the floor board until you could see the pavement. He finally had to put a piece of wood over the hole so his foot wouldn't fall through. I also remember him patching the inner tube of a tire that was completely bald, and listening to him swearing up a storm trying to get that tube back into the tire and onto the rim. But, he made do with what he had and kept on driving that car until it died and he had it towed away for junk. I'll never forget that green car with its wide white walled tires, looking like something out of the Eliot Ness era. There was some great music during the war years that will last forever, but I was too young to appreciate it. If you could analyze the music from that period, it was nothing more than the words you would find in the lonely letters written to and from the servicemen. Most of the words written in these letters were put into lyrics and music, and sung by the great male and female vocalists of the time. Once a week, I can't remember what day, the radio had a program call, "The Lucky Strike Hit Parade." Ten of the most popular songs that week were on the list and sung, starting with number ten and working up to number one. Some of the songs titles were, "I'll Be Seeing You, Faraway Places, You Belong to Me, I'll Get By and Wing and a Prayer" to name a few. The titles spoke for them selves. The Hit Parade was sponsored by the Lucky Strike Tobacco Company. The packages their cigarettes came in were green with a big red ball in the middle. As the war progressed their motto was "Lucky Strike green has gone to war." The green dye that was used in the packaging was used in the camouflage paint used by the army. After the war years, for some reason the packs stayed white with the big red ball, and never returned back to green, I wonder why. Visions and memories of the troop trains, blackout drills, POWs, Nucco and all the rest, still stay with me. As a boy I always looked at the war more or less as an exciting thing to be part of. But as I grew older I began to realize how serious war really was. I've become a big reader of books about the WWII and that four year period. I never realized how much hardship and pain was suffered by not only the people in the military, but the people at home as well. Reading about the Holocaust, prison camps, battle casualties, and seeing the soldiers on the boardwalk made it a horrible thing to remember. I was twelve when the war ended and I doubt that I understood any of the above. But, as an adult, I'm still fascinated by it all.

2-1

Aunt Vera & Uncle Wendell

M·Nr 1887715

Original German 5 Mark Note – Printed in 1908

Uncle Nick 1944
England

**5 Mark Note Printed in 1944
As Invasion Money**

**Christmas Card From Wendell
To My Grandparents 1944 France**

Armand and Margret 1942

Kriegsgefangenenpost

Postkarte

An

_____

ebührenfrei

Absender:
Vor- und Zuname:

Gefangenennummer:

S. CENSOR M. Stammlager III B
Deutschland (Allemagne)

Emplangsort:

Straße:

Land: USA
Landesteil (Provinz usw.

Kriegsgefangenenlager   Datum:

This letter was sent by my uncle to my grandparents while he was in a German POW Camp.

May 14, 1944
Dear folks just a few lines to let you know that I am doing fine and in best of health. Hoping that this card fines you all the same home. I haven't as yet received any mail from you and am anxious to hear from you. Also hoping that some day soon I can be back again. Love Armand

Nick 1943

Cousin Cousin Margret Armand Helen Anne
Wendell behind Armand 1945

CHAPTER 3
SCHOOL YEARS

When I entered the fifth grade, the war was still with us. Even though the war time memories of rationing, victory gardens, canning, war bonds and on and on were etched in my mind, I also have non war related ones as well. I remember my Uncle Angelo, who was an avid trout fisherman, giving me one of his old fly rods and taking me trout fishing for the first time. Not only was he an avid fisherman but he was also one of the most patient men I've ever known. He had taken his son Thomas and I to the North Norwich Creek where I caught my first trout. I became hooked on trout fishing from that very day. That day was the first of many more memorable days of fishing that were to come. At some time during those years, he had taken me to every trout stream in a twenty miles radius, and that's a lot of streams. Years later when, he passed away, I felt a great loss, but I still have all those memories of the times we spent together. I had another uncle, Harry, who also went trout fisherman whenever he could get the time, and I was lucky enough to go with him as well. One time that really stands out with him was when we were on our way to the Great Brook. When his car started to to heat up, the radiator flowed over just as we were ready to stop. He took a pail from the trunk of the car and walked down to the stream, got a pail of water and filled up the radiator. He put the pail back in the trunk and we walked down to the stream and started fishing. When it was time to go home, he discovered he had lost his car keys. We looked everywhere, but couldn't find them. Finally, he looked under the hood of his car, and lying on top of the battery cover were his keys. He had laid them down when he went to get the pail and forgot to pick them up. On the way home, he said he had to stop at St. Bart's Church for a minute. When I ask why, he said, he made a promise to put a dollar in the poor box if he could find the keys. Then he said, "When you make a promise, no matter to who, you keep it." I never forgot what he said, nor will I ever forget him. To me, both of these men were very special.

That was the summer I was hit by a car. I had gone on a hike with two friends to a place called the Pines. We were on our way home when we stopped on the Polkville Bridge to look at the water. I saw a big fish swimming under the bridge, and without looking, I ran across the bridge and bang. The next thing I remembered was my Mother looking down at me, and crying. I was flat on my back in the Chenango Memorial Hospital, with one leg hanging from the ceiling and a cast on my left wrist. I also had one giant sized bump on my forehead. I was laid up for over a week in that hospital before they would let me go home. While I was waiting to leave, another boy was put in the room with me. He had his thumb almost severed from his hand. He cut it while working in a silo on his farm. Later I heard the doctors were able to reattach the thumb to his hand. I didn't know him then, but eight years later the two of us would graduate from high school together. As for me, I was discharged from the hospital the next day and spent the remainder of the summer looking out the window and wishing I could go fishing.

When you're young you do some real dumb things, and I remember a lulu of one that I pulled. I was about thirteen or fourteen at the time when a boy who lived up the street from me showed me how to make a firecracker. The only thing he needed was two bolts, a nut and some wooden matches. Just about every, home in those days, had a box of wooden striking matches that were used to start their wood burning stoves. These matches had a white tip on the end and when you scraped the head across a hard surface, it would ignite the match. In essence they were just like a detonator on a bomb. If you were very careful, you could snap off the end of the white part with a knife without lighting it. He would put the nut and bolts together while carefully placing the match tips into the nut. You had to be very careful screwing the bolt down, if you didn't it might go off in your hands. He then tossed this contraption into the air and watched it come down. It hit the sidewalk just right and exploded like a firecracker. He said if he had bigger bolts he could make a blockbuster. I told him I knew where we could get real big ones. We walked down to where the roundhouse was and I showed him a pile of rails along with a pile of nuts and bolts that were used to hold railroad tracks together. These bolts had to be at least an inch and a half in diameter. We took some of the nuts and bolts back with us to my house and made a big firecracker with at least fifteen heads in it. It was too heavy to toss inknitting mill. After making sure no one was around, we climbed up to the lean-to and dropped it. When it hit the slate sidewalk, it sounded like a shotgun blast. One of the bolts left the nut and went flying through a small window in the back of the house. We were not expecting anything like that. We were scared to death that someone would show up. We just jumped off that roof and ran down an alley next to the greenhouse as fast as our legs would carry us. The next day I went over to see what happened, and found the bolt with the nut on it next to the walkway we dropped it on. I could see where the other bolt hit a wall closet door after going through that window. I hate to think what could have happened if that thing hit one of us instead of the window and wall. The funny part about the whole thing was, we didn't have to risk a broken leg jumping off that roof and running like we did. Evidently, nobody came around to investigate, and if they did, I never heard about it. The Atomic Bomb was dropped on Japan on August 6,1945 and three days later a second one was dropped. This lead to the end of the war on August 15. A few weeks later in September, I entered Junior High School. When that bomb was dropped, I was in Atlantic City visiting my Grandparents with my Aunt Vera, but for some reason I can't remember either one of them being dropped. The only memory I have at all about the bomb, at the time, was my seventh grade teacher trying to explain to the class what had happened. I doubt that any of us really understood what the bomb was all about, except that it ended the war

Junior and Senior high school were completely different from grade school. I never really had an interest in school nor did I have any lofty goals to strive for. I was only interested in having fun and just getting by in school. Besides, I wasn't that good a student, and had no real incentive at home to do well. My father wasn't the kind of person who could motivate anyone, all he would do was give a lot of criticism and very little praise. I could never go to him for help on anything. As for my mother, what she lacked in knowledge she more than made up for by just being there and making me feel better about myself when things weren't going well for me. I was too embarrassed to ask a teacher for help, which of course was very stupid on my part, because that was what they were there for. I continued to just get by in the seventh and eighth grades, and didn't wise up until I started high school. I was pretty much of a loner with very few friends when I started the junior high school. Norwich isn't very big, but it did have five small grade schools, spread around town. I spent my sixth grade at the East Main Street School before entering junior high school. When I entered junior high there were five times as many students as there were in grade school. It was only natural that I would be making more friends. I participated in school intramural sports and became a member of a team, which was a new experience for me because I was never on any kind of team. Baseball was the sport I really liked the most. In the spring, I went to watch a varsity baseball game where an older boy was keeping score for the game. He was putting all these strange symbols and numbers on a score sheet. When I asked him what they meant, he told me me every position on the team had a number assigned to it. For example, the shortstop was number six and the first baseman was number three. If the batter hit the ball to the shortstop and he threw the man out at first base, it would be scored 6-3. If some one hit a fly ball to the center fielder, it would be scored F-8, because center field was scored as number 8 and he caught the fly ball. Once I got the hang of it, I found it to be a lot of fun and you got more out of the game. I started to listen to the Brooklyn Dodger games on the radio and kept the score for the games I listening to. By the end of summer I was a full blown Dodger fan.

I was thirteen when I entered eighth grade and turning fourteen in January. I was going to need a job for the summer so I had to apply for working papers. After school was let out for the summer, I went to work picking peas and beans for one of the local farms. I would be picked up by one of their trucks every weekday morning at seven o'clock. My Mother would make me a big lunch with a big thermo of iced tea because I would be in the hot sun all day long. There were about thirty kids and a hand full of adults from Norwich, plus twice that many from the Utica area. The pickers from Utica would stay on the farm all summer long living in a place called the "Shacks" during the picking season. You would get a ticket for every bushel you brought to the loader. I'm not sure, but I think we were getting thirty cents for every bushel we picked. You could turn them in for cash any time you wanted at the farm, or if you needed something from their store, they would take the tickets in place of the cash. Each day I would give my mother the tickets and she would keep them until the end of each week when she gave them to me to cash them in. I could usually pick six to ten bushes a day, depending on the type of beans picked. She would let me keep three or four for spending money.

When I entered high school as a freshman, I still didn't know where I was heading or what I was going to do with my life after I left. I liked sports, trout fishing, the Brooklyn Dodgers, reading Hardy Boy mysteries and a passing interest in girls. I still wasn't much of an achiever in school; again, all I was doing was getting by. My sophomore year was pretty much like my freshman year, not outstanding, but I had made more friends to share my time with. I started to hang around Garff's a lot more, since this was the place to meet and see the kids from school. My friends and I would buy a coke at Garff's, cross the street and find an empty park bench and start talking to the girls as they walked by. If there was no one around, we talked macho. One of the things we did when the weather wasn't so good, was play penny poker. Four or five of us, Bub, Losky, Jim, Yac and a few others would go to someone's house and play poker until it was time to go home. By the time I was a senior I had mastered the game of stud. The following quote was in the senior class will to the junior class, which appeared in our senior class yearbook, "To the undergraduate card players we leave you Rich Biviano's thesis, "How To Win Money and Influence Poker Players."

During the winter months, I had a job at the YMCA and the Elks Club setting pins for the bowling leagues. There were no automatic pin setting machines in those days, you had to set pins by hand. I was getting good enough at it to be able to set two lanes at a time. If you were able to keep up two lanes in league play, you made three dollars for the three games. If you had a good night setting, you could make an extra fifty cents to a dollar more in tips. In the spring, I would caddie at the Canasawacta Country Club on weekends. I was getting along a lot better in school by the end of my sophomore year. I felt more relaxed, and with the new friends I had made, more secure of myself.

I went to work picking beans again that summer. The first year wasn't so bad, but the second was worse because I really didn't want to do this again. I felt like my father was right when he would say, "You'll never amount to much." I had this fixation on having a lot of friends and I thought that was all that mattered. There never was a closeness in our house, we were not what you might call a huggy, huggy, kissy, kissy family. My father didn't make it an enjoyable place to be because all he did was find fault. I was never really close with my sister Pat, although that changed later. My younger sister Barbara was only about five, and my brother Paul wasn't around yet. My mother worked all day in the Knitting Mill, but still had time to spend with me when I wanted to talk. There was a period of time when I was really down in the dumps and wanted to leave. I had asked Aunt Vera if I could live with her because things were not going well at home. She said it was OK with her if it was OK with my father. There was no way I was going to ask him, so I took the only other way out that I could think of. I kept of all the tickets I could get my hands on from picking beans, packed a small duffel bag and ran away from home. I had no idea of where I was going, I just wanted out. I left the next morning, after my Mother and Father had gone to work. Before I left I put a note on my bed saying "I'm leaving home, don't try to look for me I'll be in Canada before you read this." I walked to the outskirts of Norwich, in the opposite direction of Canada, and hitched a ride on one of the first cars that came by. That driver and his wife took me all the way to Binghamton, and now I was on my way. Luck must have been on my side that day because rides were easy to come by. The only map I had was Pennsylvania, so I headed for Pittsburgh because it was the only city I had heard of in that part of Pennsylvania. For the next few days, I just kept moving West. When I started, I had no particular place to go, I just wanted to go. Every time someone picked me up, I would tell them I was going to Pittsburgh to see my uncle or Cleveland to see my grandmother. The first day I made it into Pennsylvania and slept in an old farm barn that night. I took any ride I could get, some were only for a few miles, but others were longer. Most of the people that picked me were pretty nice and a few who were going a long distance, bought me lunch. One old couple even bought me dinner. When I wasn't treated I bought my own meals. I had put a lot of miles behind me when I was picked up by a priest and he pretty much guessed I was a runaway. He told me this was not the way to solve my problem. He strongly suggested I go back home and work things out with my family. He asked me if I had bus fare, if I didn't he'd lend me the money for the ticket. I told him I had money and promised him I would go home. He let me out at a bus stop in Vandalla, Illinois and left. I didn't want to spend money for a bus ticket so I hitchhiked back to Norwich. It took me three days and a morning to get back. It was very late when I left my ride in Binghamton so I slept on some grass behind a row of bushes. I was only forty-five miles from home, and I hitched a ride on the first car to come by the next morning, and he took me all the way to Greene, only seventeen miles from Norwich. I was stranded there for over two hours before I was finally picked up a ride the rest of the way to Norwich. When I got home, my mother was vacuuming the living room. She saw me, cried, and then hugged me tight. I hardly had time to tell her where I had gone, when my father came home for lunch. He appeared to be happy to see me back, because the first thing I remember him saying was, "Glad you finally decided to come home." That afternoon, Sheriff Macchio, a friend of my fathers came to see me. I was really scared when I saw him coming because I thought I was in deep trouble. I didn't know what he was going to do to me. I expected to get a tongue lashing, but to my surprise, he was a very understanding. First, he told me that I had caused a lot of people a lot of trouble, and that there was a three state alarm out looking for me. Then he said something I never expected, "The next time you feel like running away, give me a call and I'll help you map out a route so I'll know where you're are." I entered into my junior year that September with a new frame of mind. I was getting along a little better at home with my father. He was still the same man, but not as up tight as he once was. He still never offered much in the way of praise or encouragement, but at the same time, he wasn't criticizing as much either. I had one of the rare memorable times with my father that year. He would, on occasion be driving a man to New York City, who was receiving special medical treatments for his throat. In October of 1949, he had to make that trip again, only this time he invited me to go along. He would have to stay for four days this time, what he didn't mention before we left was he had tickets for World Series. The Brooklyn Dodgers were going to play the New York Yankees in that year and he had tickets for the first two games at Yankee Stadium. I was absolutely stunned when he told me. We sat in the right field bleachers for both games. The first game was won by the Yankees 1-0 on a home run by Tommy Henrich in the ninth inning. That ball landed about twenty feet from where I was sitting. The Dodgers won the second game by the same score of 1- 0. That was the only game the Dodgers won that year, and I got to see them play. I also got to see several of the great players in the game that year, Yogi Berra, Joe DiMaggio, Jackie Robinson and Duke Snider, to name a few.

I became more involved in school activities in my junior year. I had joined the Dramatics Club, the Thespians and I was a member of the football team until I injured the ankle that was fractured when I was hit by the car. I was voted in as the team manager for my senior year, so I was still part of the team. I believe it was my junior year when I took part in the Gilbert and Sullivan's "The Pirates of Penzance." I was a pirate, and yes, I did sing in the chorus. I was also invited by a girl to go to the Sadie Hawkins dance that year. That was the first time a girl ever asked me out on a date. We double dated with another couple, had a great time and ended up at the Bluebird Cafe after the dance. The Bluebird was the place to go after a date or just to have a cup of coffee. You could always be sure to see somebody there. I remember when four or five of us used to go there after school a lot. In those, you could play a record on the jukebox for nickel, and for a quarter you could get six plays. We would put the quarter in and play the same record over and over and over. The record was "The Syncopated Clock," and it used to drive the waitresses crazy. They couldn't wait for us to leave. I never really liked the taste of coffee, it was just something to do. I remember putting two spoons of sugar and two half and half creamers in it just to make it taste better. This would change when I went into the Navy.

In the winter time, if it were cold enough, the city would flood the park in front of the old high school. By the next day, it would be frozen hard enough to skate on and presto, we had ice skating rink. It was just another place for the kids to meet and socialize. I would also like to state here that drugs were non existence when I was in school, if they were around, I never saw them. The only time you heard anything about drugs was in the movies when somebody would mentioned something about the opium trade. As I remember, this was referred to when the setting of the movie was in the Orient. The only other references to a narcotic were people who smoked reefers. I never saw one, but I understand they was used by musicians and unsavory characters. Words like crack, uppers, downers and cocaine weren't in our vocabulary. Coke was something you bought at Garff's for a nickel to drink, not smoke.

During my junior-senior summer I got my first real job with a paycheck. I worked for the Chenango County Highway Department cutting grass, with a scythe blade, along the county highways. I was part of a four man team, of which three of us were high school students. I can tell you there is nothing as brutal as cutting tall dry grass under a humid, blistering sun along the highways for eight hours a day. That summer couldn't get over fast enough for me, but it sure was better than picking beans. One of the first things I bought with some of the money I put away, was a pair of white buck shoes, which were considered "cool" back then. My senior year was a blast for me. I had made lots of friends, and my attitude towards school changed. The Korean War was on and I knew what I was going to do when I graduated. I know this might not seem like a lofty ambition, but you must remember I was seventeen going on eighteen with little home direction. But before this, there was still my senior year. I was the boy's sports' editor on the school paper, the High Tribune," and our year book, the Archive. This was in addition to the other clubs that I was in. I was very excited about the idea of getting my first driver's license. I couldn't wait for the test, but at the time driver training was just coming into its' own and I had to wait my turn. But eventually it came and I took and passed the test the first time. After getting the license, I didn't have a car to drive and I knew my Father wasn't going to let me use his without a lecture. When Junior Prom time came, I asked him if I could use the car, and to my complete surprise, he said yes, but with the expected lecture, I had anticipated. I must add here that the music in the early fifties were full of great songs and singers. I can still hear Nate King Cole singing Mona Lisa, Too Young and Unforgettable while Patti Page was singing the Tennessee Waltz. These and others blended in with the music of the 40s. Not only was it great music to dance to, it was also great listening music. But how could it not have been great listening, when you had Frank Sinatra, Doris Day, PerryComo, and Dean Martin to name a few. We also had a lot of fun songs like "Mister Sandman, Four Leaf Clover and how could I overlook Sh-Boom Sh-Boom. We didn't have hard rock or rap music, we had, and I say this with tongue in cheek, "classy music." There were the unforgettable classics like Mirzy-Doats, The Woody Woodpecker Song, The Purple People Eater, the Maharajah of Magadore and Phil Harris singing "The Thing." One of the craziest songs was Spike Jones and His City Slickers singing "Tea for Two." I know the waitresses at the Bluebird will always remember some of us from the class of 51 because of the Syncopated Clock. And I seriously believe the 50s had the greatest music for slow dancing that was ever written. I still remember the night, sitting in Frank's car in front of his house along with Mike, drinking beer and telling dirty jokes. We were laughing so loud, that Frank's Sister Louise came out and told us to go home before somebody calls the cops. Writing about this made me smile and brought to mind another story these two and a few others were involved in. Another one of our friends used to drive his fathers' panel truck to school once on a while. After school one day five or six of us got into the back of the truck and lit up some God awful cigars with the windows closed to see who would be the first one to leave. I can't remember which one of us was the first, it may even have been a five-way tie, but my eyes smarted of two hours afterwards. Smoking cigarettes and cigars was not my thing. But, I saw actors smoking in the movies and thought that was cool. When I finally tried it, all I could do was choke and gag on the smoke. One of my friends said if you inhaled, you would enjoy it more. I tried it, didn't like it, and choked some more. I may not have been the greatest student in school, but I did manage to graduate. With that honor, if that's what you call it, went the family title of "First grandchild to graduate on either side of the family from high school." I didn't particularly want to go to college, but if I had, there wasn't money to send me. Besides, I had Korea on my mind, and wanted to be a hero like my uncles and cousins before me. Without my parents knowing it, in May of '51, I went to Binghamton along with a few others from my class and enlisted in the navy. I was told by the recruiter I had to wait until I graduated and would be contacted by mail when to report. It was now time for me to drop this bomb shell on the family. A couple of days after graduation I received the anticipated letter and told my parents what I had done. I remember my mother cried, and my father said "I hope you know what your doing." After telling them, the word was out that I was going into the Navy. I didn't know it at the time but a big party was being planned by a few of my friends, under the pretense of going out for a pizza with Barney, Dave, Bub and a few others who came to my house to pick me up. This turned into the biggest party I had ever been to. Half of the guys in my class turned out. We met at a place call Quacks for one big beer blast with lots of beer, pizza, and burgers. After the last beer, I vaguely remember throwing up in the local drive in theater and later waking up at Chenango Lake in Barney's family cottage, along with at least twelve other guys sleeping on the floor. Boy did I ever have a big head in the morning. When I got home my father asked me how I felt. Barney's father had called him earlier that morning to tell him where I was. He also knew about the party before I did, and figured I was there when I didn't come home at night. I will never forget that going away party or the guys who were there. Years later when I started to attend my class reunions, this was the topic of conversation at the earlier ones.

Stan – Frankie – Buzz – Joe – Me – Frank – 1951

Me – Frank 1950

Boy Scouts – 1948
Frank – Barney – Me – Joe
Carmen – Dick – Ed – John - Rich

Celebrating Graduation
With the Champaign of bottled beer.
Bub-Me-Dave-Jim-Barney-Arch- Norm

RICHARD BIVIANO
RICH—"A man and his dream" . . .
curly black hair . . . an avid sports
writer . . . Miss Carey's right-hand
man . . . a practical joker . . . 'fun
where you find it' . . . unpredictable
moods . . . a Dodger fan.

Class Year Book

2

Photo of Bluebird Café Painting By Ruby Crespell

Me & Ward

Me – Jim (back)
Bub – Guy (front)
New York weekend
Senior year

Christmas Formal 1950

TheOld High School
Now an Office Building

CHAPTER 4
U.S. NAVY

The closer I got to leaving for the Navy, the more excited I became. I was so hopped up about going, I just couldn't wait until I got to Boot Camp. I no longer wanted to be in the army as I had envisioned when I was younger, because the navy seemed like a more exciting choice. The Naval recruiter told me I was accepted and would be reporting to the Naval Training Center in Great Lakes, Illinois in July. I would be contacted with the date and details by mail. In the mean time I was to go back to school and graduate. I didn't need my parents' signature because I was eighteen and didn't need my parent's approval. I kept this from them until after the graduation exercises. I was finally contacted by the navy and told to report to the Naval Training Center in Great Lakes, Illinois via railroad. On July 23 Barney and two other friends picked me up at my house and drove me to Sidney, N.Y. where I was to meet the train for Great Lakes. When the train arrived, a sailor with a clipboard called my name, along with several others who were waiting, and we boarded the train that started my great adventure. We made several other stops on our way to Chicago picking up more enlistees as we went along. When we arrived at the training center we were met by two petty officers who were yelling and screaming at us to get aboard the buses as they called our names. No matter how fast we moved, it wasn't fast enough. I'm not sure what I was thinking at that moment, but it had to be "What the hell am I doing here?" Remember me saying how excited I was to get to Boot Camp? Guess what, I lost the excitement twenty minutes after I got there. The boot camp lasted sixteen weeks, and there was someone always screaming at us to hurry up. They cut my hair bald, made me take calisthenics every morning, and then it was nothing but work day after day. If it wasn't marching, it was drilling, or the rifle range, and when we finished, there might be a field day in the barracks. In between these little chores we were going to school for classes on naval nomenclature, semaphore, naval history, hygiene and the U. S. Code of Military Justice (The Blue Jacket Manual). We went to fire fighting classes, swimming classes, abandon ship drills, and on and on and on, and it never seemed to stop. One of the first things we had to learn was how to drill, that's marching to you civilians. The first day on the drill field was a joke. Half of the guys had no idea on how to keep up with the cadence. Our drill instructor was a marine drill sergeant who spoke to us in a voice that was very loud, clear, and with single words stating "You-will-learn-how-to-march-properly." If-you-don't,-your-ass-is-grass-and-I'm-the-lawn-mower," Pause, "Do-you-understand-me?" Some of the guys from New York City didn't know right from left, and we all paid the price. This drill sergeant was the most sadistic person I had ever in met in my short life. He made us stand, with our arms extended out in front of us with the rifle laying on the top of our fists. We stood there for a minute or so, and we all began to falter, but no one dared to drop their weapon. I can tell you that everyone knew his left from his right after that little exercise, and cadence became easier after that. This man also used some of the foulest language I had ever heard.

We marched everywhere, to chow, classes, swimming, even to church. The marching, along with a good diet of food, lots of sleep, lights out in the barracks at nine and an early morning reveille put us in pretty good shape after a couple of weeks. Reveille was at five o'clock sharp with our barracks commander banging the inside of a forty-five gallon trash can with a wooden bat. It's a wonder someone didn't have a heart attack or go insane. We all had thirty minutes to shower, shave and get dressed in the uniform of the day. After this it was clean up the barracks time, which had to be done by six-thirty so we could line up outside of the barracks and march to breakfast by seven. After breakfast we were marched back to our barracks for inspection and then marched again to our first class of the day. This routine was repeated every day for sixteen weeks.

Halfway through boot camp we were given a twenty-four pass on Sunday. Our company commander, first class petty officer Stump, impressed upon us the importance of getting back on time for muster the next morning. He wasn't exactly polite in telling us this, because every other word that came out of his mouth was a threat, because he wanted to make sure we understood. Me and two friends of mine decided we should go together since none of us had ever been to Chicago, this way we were sure of getting back on time. This was a new experience for me, because I had never really spent any time in a big city except for when I went to New York City with my father for the World Series. Getting away from Stump and boot camp for few hours was the best thing that could have happened to us. Getting yelled at all the time gets to be a real drag. By the time my training was over, I began to realize why he acted the way he did. We were just a bunch of wise guys fresh out of high school with little contact with the real world. I think part of it was to make us understand we would be acting as a team once we left here, and were assigned to duty, and he only a short time to get this point across to us. What ever the reason, I think I came out of boot camp a more disciplined person then when I went in. The days seemed to last forever, much like picking beans and peas, but the sixteen weeks went by fast. After graduation we were given a fourteen day leave. I called my parents to tell them I was coming home and that I had already made arrangements for a ride home from Binghamton with Barney and Yac. Once I arrived home all my uncles, aunts and cousins showed up to welcome me home. A couple of my uncles, who had been in the army, asked how I liked boot camp, they all had smiles on their faces when they asked. I just smiled back and shook my head. It was great to be home. The two weeks went by too fast for me, between visiting family members, parties and getting together every night was burning my two weeks leave fast. But I enjoyed every day and hour it. I missed my Mom a lot, but I didn't see my Father much while I was home. He was working days, and seemed to have a lot of things to do at night. But we managed to get along for the short time that I was home. I was now looking forward to Great Lakes and what my new assignment would be. Before I left to come home from boot camp, I had to fill out a form asking for my first three choices of duty. I was told that it didn't mean I would get what I wanted, but they wanted to know. I had asked for a school for radar, radio or sonar, and a destroyer, aircraft carrier or a cruiser, all in that order. When I returned from leave, I was given an envelope with orders and a train ticket, with instructions to report to the destroyer USS Ross DD563 in Long Beach, California in four days.

The ship was just coming out of the mothball fleet, where it was put after World War II, and waiting to be activated for duty with the fleet in the future. I went aboard as a radioman striker, but didn't see the inside of a radio shack for over a month. I was instead assigned to the deck force to chip paint. That was hard noisy work for six to seven hours a day. Little by little I managed to get to the radio shack where I met the men I would eventually work with. They helped me with the code, how to handle the key, and showed me some of the equipment I would be using. I finally got assigned to the radio room only to be, you guessed it, chipping paint. I learned fast that the low man in the pecking order gets the worse jobs. After activating the Ross we went on our first shake cruise, after we were transferred to the fleet in San Diego. This was also where I would spend my first Christmas away from home.

We were only going to be at sea, on the short shake down, for the day. The experience I had that day will never be forgotten. We may only have been going for the day, but the moment we left the pier I became a little woozy. Before I- knew it I ran to the head and tossed up everything I had for this morning's breakfast and last night's dinner. I was so sea sick I thought I was going to die. And if that wasn't bad enough, later I got the dry heaves. I wouldn't wish seasickness on my worse enemy. I takes a while to get over this sickness even though you never really get over it. I never acquired a taste for coffee prior to joining the navy. The only time I drank it was when I was with my friends sitting in a booth at the Bluebird Cafe. In most movies about the navy you always see a sailor with a mug of coffee in his hands. They weren't drinking it, they were keeping their hands warm with it. I know that, because that's what I did with it when I had the watch at sea. Later, out of boredom I would sip it because it was hot, eventually I was drinking it on a regular basis. Another thing I never did before enlisting was smoking cigarettes. This was a habit I also picked up out of shear boredom while at sea. The fact that I was able to buy them in the ships' store for eighty cents a carton made it even easier. Before I knew it, I was smoking a pack a day.

In March of 1952 the Ross was finally out of moth balls and ready to join the fleet. Our first assignment was to escort the USS Ticonderoga and USS Intrepid, both WWII aircraft carriers that served in the pacific, to the East Coast via the Panama Canal. I think they were going to New York for overhaul, but I'm not sure. Going through the canal was a real treat and an exciting adventure for me. I remember seeing movies and reading about the building of the canal and the hardships, along with malaria, suffered by the builder. Once you go through the canal locks and enter Gatun Lake you notice there are no cities or rest stops, it was nothing but jungle as far as you can see. We stayed in Cristobel for a few days and then on to Norfolk., Virginia. While here, I was sent to radio school in Bainbridge, Maryland. After spending three months in radio school, it was back to Norfolk and the Ross. Shortly after returning from school we made a cruise to Guantanamo Bay, Cuba for more training, fleet exercises and gunnery practice. When we returned to Norfolk we received word that we were going on a midshipmen cruise to Northern Europe. We would be taking ROTC (Reserve Officers Training Corp) students aboard for the trip. Before leaving for the cruise, I went home on a long week end pass and learned my very close friend Frank, who had joined the Marine Corp the same day I signed up for the navy, was killed in Korea. Frank had gotten married while I was at sea and I never got the chance to congratulate him and his new bride. I never had the chance to congratulate them or see him again. I remember feeling so very bad about Frank and wanted to talk to his wife Frances, but couldn't get the courage to call her while I was home.

I had just gone through the Panama Canal, and now I was going to Europe, how lucky can you be. Traveling to Europe for the first time was a very special thing for me. I had never been further from home then New Jersey before I joined up, but now I was going to see Londonderry, Ireland, Edinburgh, Scotland and Oslo, Norway. I soon found out that the anticipation was greater then the experience. I don't remember much about Ireland except for tasting my first glass of a very strong ale called Guinness Stout. After drinking it for the first time, I can't remember ever having a glass of it again. The real truth is I hated it the first time. On our stop in Edinburgh, Scotland, John, one of my friends aboard ship, had a grandmother living in the village of Cowdenbluth, I'm not sure of the spelling. He had gotten permission to leave the area to visit her, and invited another friend Dave and myself to go along. The train ride was worth the price of admission, and better than any bus tour we could have taken. Her home and the town itself was something out of the John Wayne movie called "The Quiet Man." To see him meeting his Grandmother was well worth the trip. The next day we all got to visit the city of Edinburgh and another first for me, I had my first taste of Drambuie. I never was a big drinker then, and today I seldom drink at all, but a bottle of the Scotch Liqueur Drambuie has been in my house since the day I was married. On our way to Norway via the North Sea we could see the fjords all the way to Oslo, where we would be for the next two days. We had liberty as soon as we arrived, so John, Dave and I hopped a cable car ride to the top of the mountain to see the Holmenkollen Ski Jump where the the 1952 Winter Games were held. We also got to see the original Kon Tiki Raft that was on exhibit at the Oslo Museum. In case you had never heard of this raft, six men floated on it from Peru across, the Pacific Ocean to the islands around Tahiti. Historians were trying to prove a theory that these islands could have been discovered by Peruvian natives with the use of a raft built similar to this one. I got to see a lot of interesting things in Oslo in the little time I was there, but the navy said it was time to go hone.

After returning from the midshipmen cruise I was notified that my Grandfather had passed away and I was given a five day leave to attend the funeral. Little did I know I was was about to meet the girl I would be spending the rest of my life with. After the funeral I was introduced to Marie, the girl he would marry, and her sister Jo. There were no arrows shot through my heart by Cupid, no fireworks, no nothing that would indicate spending the rest of my life with her. At first I thought she was a just a fresh snot as well as a bore. At the time, the only reason I ever saw her at all was because my cousin would invite me to go with them for a pizza or see a movie or just walk the boards. Since I didn't know anyone else in Atlantic City, it was logical that I would go out with them. There were three important events leading up to my meeting and eventually marrying Jo. These events were death, fire and storm. I named them the "Four Horses of the Apocalypse," My Grandfather's funeral was the first one.

When my leave was up, I returned to Norfolk and the Ross. A few months later, I took my first leap into the world of debt. While on a weekend pass to Norwich I saw a 1949 Mercury that I wanted. I was tired of hitch hiking rides home whenever I had a week end pass. When I went back to the ship I made the arrangement for the payment to be taken from my pay. I quickly found out there was more to buying a car than the payments, namely gas, insurance, repairs, and on and on and on. This was probably good training for me for when I would be getting married.

After a few months, the Ross was moved to the Philadelphia Navy Yard for a major overhaul. My Aunt Margaret was living in South Philly at the time so I spent the nights there instead of the barracks barracks in the shipyard. She was only a fifteen minute ride to the ship yard by subway. While in Philadelphia I started going to Atlantic City for the weekends and naturally my cousin would fix me up on occasion with a date with Jo. Four months later the Ross returned to Norfolk and the fleet. We made one short cruise to Guantanamo Bay, Cuba for a shake down and then back to Norfolk. Shortly after returning, I was transferred to the USS Ingram DD-694 where I finished out my tour of duty. I was discharged from the Navy on July 22, 1955 and placed into the inactive Naval Reserves for four years. I didn't receive my final discharge until 1959.

During my tour with the Ross, I traveled to Northern Europe, the Med, The Caribbean, South America and, up and down the Atlantic and Pacific Coasts. I visited more countries in that four years then most people had seen in a life time. I got to see Spain, Ireland, Scotland, Norway, the Azores, Venezuela, Panama, Cuba and Jamaica.

I never saw or took part in any battles I had hoped for when I was a youngster. I never got the chance to experience what my uncles had in WWII, but as I look on it today I'm sure they would probably have said "Richard, you don't know how lucky you were." I enjoyed my time on the Ross, it was exciting being on a ship that once took part in the battles for Saipan, Tinian, Eniwetok, the Marianas, Peleliu, and the Solomon's. The ship earned five battle stars for her part in the war. Several years ago I came upon a book entitled "Destroyer Saga" A Journal of war and a sinking ship written by Ben Coe the first commanding Officer of the Ross. It gave me a detailed account of what happened to the ship in October, 1944 when she ended up in a mine field hitting a mine, and little later hitting a second one. After being towed to an anchorage for repairs she was again hit, this time by a Japanese plane, and four days later by a kamikaze causing more death and destruction to the Ross and its crew. I felt myself being there, but was glad I wasn't. There were times aboard ship that weren't as exciting as others, and there was also a lot of boredom when you were at sea, but then again I wasn't on a cruise ship. I never did distinguish myself with heroic acts of bravery, but as I look back on it, it was a great adventure and experience for me. Even though I didn't spend much time in the places that the ship dropped anchor, I had seen enough to make me want to see more. As a result, I was bitten by the travel bug, which I sill have today. Spending four years in the Navy was probably the best thing that could have happened to me. I have the self esteem now that I didn't have when I joined, and I think I was better equipped to face the real world then instead of when I graduated from high school, with no real plan for the future.

4-1

Boot Camp Great Lakes, Ill – 1951

Boot Camp Liberty with
Friends in Chicago - 1951

Hot Shot Radiomen

Getting Some Sun and
Taking it Easy at Sea

Opening Doors to Next Lock

4-2

Jamaica – 1952

Oslo Norway

Salty Sailors

USS Ross DD563

"Mechanical Mule"
Used to Pull Ship into Next Lock

CHAPTER 5
COURTSHIP & MARRIAGE

I was discharged from the Navy in July 1955, and ready to join the civilian world. I still didn't have a real plan as to what I would do when I left. First, I went home to see the family and relax for a few days before deciding what I was going to do. After visiting with everyone I started looking a job in the Norwich and Binghamton areas, but there were none to be had, so after another tearful good bye by my Mother, I left for Philadelphia to stay with my aunt and uncle. I had asked them, when I was stationed in Philadelphia, if I could stay with them for a while after I was discharged to look around for work if I couldn't find something home. Except for being a radioman in the navy, I had no real marketable skills, so I had to take pot luck on a job. I ran across an ad in the Philadelphia Bulletin that read, "Young man needed to do ship's typing and detailing, experience not necessary, will train, or words to that effect. I thought since I had put four years in the Navy as a radioman I could probably do the job. I called and got the interview only to find out there was an error in the ad. The ad should have read "ship's piping" not "ship's typing," in other words a draftsman to make detail drawings. When I told the interviewer I had taken two years of mechanical drawing classes in high school, he said that was enough and offered me the job for $1.50 an hour. That sounded good enough to me, I was only making a hundred and fifteen dollars a month in the navy. The following Monday morning I showed up at the J.J. Henry Co. ready for work. After doing this for a few weeks, I thought this was something I might like to do for a living. I enrolled in the Temple University Engineering School, to study mechanical design at night under the GI Bill. It was still summertime and Atlantic City was only sixty miles away, so I decided to spend a weekend at the shore. Jo and I crossed paths again and before I knew it I was spending all of my weekends there. I would work Monday through Friday, rush to my aunt's house for a change of clothes and headed to the shore. By the time September rolled around I was going to school three nights a week and cramming my homework into all the spare time that was left. Between this and my work schedule it seemed like I was always tired, so I stopped going to the shore every weekend, but managed to go on an occasional Sunday. I spent Thanksgiving at the shore that first year, but when Christmas came I went home to see my family. In January my cousin Bob and Marie had set a date in August for their wedding, and were having a party at the Stanley Restaurant in Atlantic City to celebrate. Jo and I were driving around looking for a place to park that was close to the restaurant, when we spotted a space in front of a church. I wasn't sure if it was a legal parking space, but, I parked there anyway. The two of sat in the car for a while talking about getting married. All of a sudden out of nowhere came the sounds of a police car siren followed by fire trucks. The church we were parked in front of burst into flames and we got out of there quick like a bunny. After finding another parking spot we went directly the restaurant. Bob and Marie were to be married in August, and after discussing this with Jo's parents, it was decided we would be married the following September. On March seventeenth Jo's parents gave us an engagement party which was also at the Stanley Restaurant. The weather that night turned into the biggest snow storm in Atlantic City history at the time. Think about that, we meet at a funeral, we decide to get married, and a church burst into flames and then the snow storm of the century when Jo gets her ring. I mentioned earlier about the Four Horsemen of the Apocalypse. I asked myself, "Is this an Omen of things to come?" We were married on September 22, 1956 in Ste. Michaels Church on Mississippi Ave. in Atlantic City without the fourth horseman following me with another unforgettable event. We were married by a new Priest, who was performing his first Marriage Ceremony. Afterwards I asked him if he had done everything right, he laughed and said yes, while nodding his head. I'm sure he did everything right because we celebrated our fifty-fourth anniversary this past September. After the reception, we left for a four day honeymoon at Lake George in upstate New York, and from there to our new apartment in Philadelphia.

We signed a lease effective September 1 to give us time to get our new apartment ready for us when we returned from the honeymoon. Our landlord had finished painting the apartment just before we rented it, but Jo didn't like the colors because they wouldn't go with the furniture, curtains and decorations she had decided on. We asked the landlord if we could repaint the walls a different color, he said we could, but we had to buy our own paint and paint the walls ourselves. Between working all day, going to school nights, looking for furniture and painting, my time was at a premium. But somehow it was finished just a few days before the wedding. When I was finished we were very pleased with ourselves on the way it turned out. When we entered the apartment for the first time after returning from Lake George, we found a sign on our kitchen table that read "WELCOME TO YOUR NEW HOME." The sign had dollar bills folded into ribbons surrounding it. We were not expecting this from our landlord who didn't even know us. This was an older neighborhood and I guess they were just glad to have young people in the house.

I was working as a detail draftsman at an engineering company in Philadelphia, and Jo had a job with an insurance company as an illustrator. Marriage was a new experience for me and the first thing I learned was you never have much money left at the end of the week. I guess you might say we were as poor as church mice. We decided the first thing we had to do with our paychecks was to pay the rent, and buy enough tokens to get us back and forth to work on the subway. Whatever was left, paid for the phone bill, utilities and food. I remember we ate a lot of small meals. In all fairness to Jo, she was one of the shrewdest shoppers I've ever seen. Taking her to the local supermarket for groceries was an education in frugality, if there is such a word. She always had a pocket full of coupons and spent a lot of time comparing prices. If an off brand can of beans was three cents less, this was what we got. By payday we didn't have a dollar between us, we were always broke, about the only thing we could afford to do was watch television, play Scrabble or 500 rummy. I was pretty good playing rummy and won most of the time. Playing Scrabble was different story because Jo ran circles around me in this game. After we finished playing I would put the final score on the inside cover of the Scrabble box. We still have that original scrabble game and the cover with all the scores and I'm sad to say I lost eighty present of the time. Thanksgiving being a four day holiday, meant that we would be driving to Norwich for the long weekend. The '49 Mercury, I bought while in the Navy, was on its' last leg, There were all kinds of problems with this car, but the biggest was tires. All we ever bought were used bald or recapped tires to replace the bald tires we already had, but they kept us going. The trip to Norwich was always an adventure when it came to the tires. Before leaving, I had to make sure my bald spare tire and another bald tire that was mounted on a spare rim in my trunk were holding air. We didn't have the Northeast extension of the turnpike or Rte. 81 to travel on, what we had was the infamous rte. 611 all the way to Binghamton. Between changing a tire and driving a two lane highway the entire way, the trip took over nine hours to get there. Today I drive this trip in less then five hours. The following year we managed to buy another car, going from trading our '49 Mercury for a '50 Buick. All we did was jump out of the frying pan into the fire, because that car didn't last very long either, but it was better than the Mercury. After returning from Norwich we bought our first Christmas tree. The front room in our apartment wasn't very big, so we bought a three foot high silver aluminum tree. We put it on an end table and decorated it with one string of lights and a box of Christmas balls.

I have very few vices in my life and fishing was the big one, I felt if I could get Jo interested, I'd have the perfect marriage. One evening after dinner, I suggested we go fishing Saturday morning and afterwards we could drive to to the shore and spend the rest of the day visiting with her parents. She wasn't crazy about the fishing part, but said she would go. When the alarm rang at 4:30 AM I started to hear mumbles of regret, my great idea was starting to unravel. The ride to the lake only took about forty five minutes, but it was a long quiet forty five minutes. I knew someone who rented boats at the lake by the day on the honor system. I picked up a set of oars that were under the back porch of his cottage and few minutes later we were in the boat and on or way. We had been on the water for about a half hour when I heard the first complaint, "I'm bored." Ten minutes later I heard, "I'm cold," a few minutes later, "I'm hungry," and again a little later, "How much longer are we going to stay?" After this, it was the final complaint, "I have to pee." I turned the boat around, rowed back to the dock, put the oars back and put the money for the boat inside the door. I put my gear in the car and never said another word all the way to the Ventnor. Needless to say, I never asked her again, so much for my great idea. There was another time when I tried to get her to go to a ball game with me. I bought two tickets to see the Phillies play the Dodgers, hoping to get her interested in sports. The game lasted about three hours, and all she knew at the end of the game was the blue team (Dodgers) were playing the red team (Phillies). Again, she was bored, hungry, tired and of course she made at least three trips to the ladies room with me escorting her each time. At this point I would like to give some advice to any young man who is thinking of marriage to consider this advice very carefully. You must find out if you're intended likes sports, fishing, golf, the outdoors and especially, sitting around doing nothing on a Sunday afternoons. If she doesn't, take a long second look before committing yourself, or better yet call Dr. Phil."

Philadelphia is a big city in a big state and Norwich is a little town in a big state. To bump into a friend on any street in Norwich would be a common occurrence, but what are the odds of meeting someone from Norwich in a city of millions? I was walking up the steps from the subway on my way home from work when a voice called out "Hey, Richie." I turned and saw an old friend from Norwich who I used to play Monopoly with. I hadn't seen him since I left to join the Navy. After both of us bringing each other up to date, I invited him and his girlfriend to come visit with us that evening. They were living in an apartment just six blocks from where we were. That was the beginning of a renewed friendship that was not to last long. He and his girlfriend would come over every

Friday night to play Scrabble with us. This went on for about a year until one evening his girlfriend called to tell us he had died from some kind of a virus. He was only twenty-six years old.

We were going on our second year in the apartment when Jo became pregnant. I remember her waking me up and saying it was time to go. It caught me by complete surprise at four o'clock in the morning. I was so nervous I forgot what I was supposed to do, but I managed to get her to the Einstein Medical Center in nothing flat, luckily our apartment was only three blocks away. I sat in the waiting room for over an hour before the doctor came out and told me everything was going fine and I should go home and get some sleep, and he would call me when it was time. All I could think of was, is it a boy or girl, was Jo alright, what's taking so long, and why doesn't someone call me. Finally around noon I get the call that I'm the father of a baby boy, born at 11:45 A.M. on July 1, 1958, tipping the scale at four pounds and fifteen ounces. A half hour later I was looking at him through the window in the nursery. Pinned on the basket was the name Michael, the name we had decided on if it were a boy. On the way home after seeing him I stopped at the Woolworth Store to buy him his first toy, a wind up tractor with rubber lugs, I guess I wasn't thinking because it would be a long time before he was able to play with a toy like that. Being a father for the first time is a new experience, and you have no clue of how to do anything for him. I remember pinning a diaper on him and having it fall off when I picked him up, because I didn't pin the two ends of the diaper together. Today you don't put diapers on with a safety pin you put them on with Velcro. I was never happy about changing his diaper in the first place, particularly after a messy number two that had a stench that would gag a maggot, but in spite of this unpleasant chore I learned to accept it. The only other thing that was hard for me to cope with was his crying. I always felt so helpless because I didn't know what he wanted or what to do for him. But, I could love a little more if he had been house broken and could talk.

We celebrated our first Christmas as a family of three in 1958, using the same silver tree from our first Christmas. I added another box of Christmas balls and an angel on the top. We still have a few of the Christmas balls from that first tree and I still use them today.

Our landlord, the Poppers, adored Michael, and every chance they got they wanted to hold him or baby sit for us while we went out. One day when I stopped to pay the rent, Mr. Proper said he thought it was time for us to buy a house. He said the rent we were paying could very easily be a mortgage payment. He also made it very clear that we could there stay as long as we wanted, but it was foolish to pay him rent if we could have our own home. I discussed this idea with Jo, and we both thought the idea made a lot of sense. When spring came, we started driving around the South Jersey area on weekends looking at houses. After several weeks of looking we found a new development being built in Mantua called Center City. There were seven sample sample homes that were built for you to look at and go through. We picked a three bedroom split level without a garage for $9,990. If we wanted an attached garage, it would cost $500 more, so we opted for the no garage deal to hold our monthly payment down. Remember, these were in 1959 dollars. They had a layout of the development in the office showing exactly where every home was located. The one we picked would be ready for occupancy in about six weeks. There were no paved streets as yet, but there were houses in this area that were already occupied. We drove to where ours was located, but all we could see now was the foundation and the basic frame of the house. We were very excited about the new house, and every weekend we would drive to the development to see how much progress was being made. Each weekend we could see the house in different stages and started talking about what we would need once we moved in. We had furniture for the bedroom, kitchen and living room but we needed more than a just a crib for Michael's room that became our first priority. Finally the house was ready for us to move in, but we had a little hitch. The week before we were to make settlement at the bank, I was laid off. Everything we had was put into this house and I wasn't about to tell the bank. I had two weeks pay and vacation time coming so we weren't completely broke just a little bent. This may have taken some of the enjoyment out of our moving, but we waited too long for this moment to stop now. We made settlement and the three of us moved into our new home without a job.

5-1

Uncle Nick's Band

A. C. Beach - 1956

Jo & Father Leaving for Church

Jo – Marie

Best Man & Me

Norwich on Three Spares

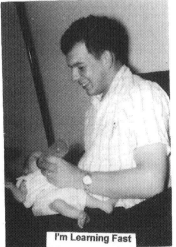

Honeymoon – Lake George

The Wedding is Finally over

Mike - First Christmas

Mike last day in Apt

I'm Learning Fast

First Day In new House

Jersey Girl To Become Bride of Richard T. Biviano

Mr. and Mrs. Domenic Albertis, of 11 N. Nashville Avenue, Ventnor City, N. J., have announced the engagement of their daughter, Josephine Jean, to Richard Thomas Biviano, son of Mr. and Mrs. Patsy Biviano of 11 Griffin Street, Norwich.

Miss Albertis is a graduate of Atlantic City High School, and is employed at Ann's Beauty Shop, her parents' establishment.

Mr. Biviano is a graduate of Norwich High School and is attending Temple University and is also employed by the United Engineers in Philadelphia.

No date has been set for the wedding.

50

CHAPTER 6
THE FIRST HOUSE

We left a lot of memories in our Grange Street apartment, the friendships of Mr. and Mrs. Propper, the Greenbergs our next door neighbors and the young couple Lucy, Tony and their new son Anthony who lived across from us. The excitement of having Michael and now a new house was all we talked and thought about. A few days before we were to move in, there had been a heavy rain fall. Madison Ave, our street, was paved only to the intersection of the street on our corner. From there down, the street was a sea of mud. The curbs were the only thing that had been pored with concrete before the heavy rains. When the moving van arrived with our belongings, the builder had to lay sheets of plywood all the way from the van to our front door, while our movers covered the new rugs and stairway with tarps to help keep the mud to a minimum. There were four other houses next to and across from us that were occupied. The rest of the houses on the street were either waiting for the new owners to move in or were in the finished stages. One of the women, Ethel, who lived directly across from us, came over to introduce herself. She had three small children and told us she had been living with dust and mud for the past two weeks waiting for the street to be paved. A week after we moved in, the builders finished paving the sidewalks, curbs and driveways, making every occupied house on the block happy.

I never had to apply for unemployment before, and it was a blow to my ego. I was determined to find a job somewhere and every morning I left the house with a handful of resumes and a list of every engineering company in South Jersey and Philadelphia. While I was job hunting, a telephone was being installed in our new kitchen and that afternoon I received a call from the Warren Webster Co. in Camden. I was a little puzzled because I hadn't left a resume there. One of my old supervisors had a neighbor who was the chief engineer with the company and looking for a tool designer. He had built me up with a great recommendation for the position. I went for the interview the next day, showed my resume, talked for a while and got the job. I was to report to work the first of the month. I was told by the interviewer that they were waiting for my phone to be installed. They actually had my phone number before I did, and that job interview couldn't have come at a better time.

We were really strapped for money that first year because the lay off had taken a bigger toll than I had thought. For us, money was as scarce as water on a desert. The eighty dollar mortgage payment, utilities, and gas money getting to and from work was eating up over half of my monthly take home. We had to find a way to make that money stretch another year. I couldn't take a second job because I was going to school three nights a week. I'm going to tell you one of the ways, which may not have been morally correct, but you "got to do what you gotta do." I had applied for six different gas credit cards and put them to work. I would use card A to charge gas for the next month, and then begin using card B the next month. By then the bill would come in for card A and I wouldn't pay it until they sent a second notice, then I would send a payment just before the cancellation date which made my credit good again with them. I would continue with card B until the same thing happened, etc. etc. etc. We were doing this for the better part of a year without ever missing a payment. We kept this up until I finally got my first raise. It may not have been the right thing to do, and I'm not recommending anyone doing this, believe me, it was nerve racking along with a bit of guilt feeling thrown in. We had some lean years after that, but most of the friends we had made in the development were pretty much in the same boat. Our entertainment consisted primarily of playing cards and visiting each other. Movies and going out to dinner were not meant to be, this was considered a luxury we couldn't afford, but things eventually got better. We now had hospitalization, paid vacations and sick time, which was something we never had while in the job shops.

We needed to have a garage, if for nothing else than to store the lawnmower, beach chairs, bicycles, and all the other junk that we didn't have room for inside. I didn't have the money to buy all of the materials I needed to build it. However, I found a way to get all of the siding I needed. Warren Webster had eight foot pieces of copper tubing shipped to them in wooden boxes made of 1 x 8 pine wood crating. I got permission to take a many of these crates as I wanted, and with the help of a friend who had a station wagon, took several of these home every day after work. It took a lot of trips to get enough wood to build a one car garage, but getting them was one thing, taking them apart was another. Every box had to be taken apart without breaking the wood, and after that the nails had to come out. This required a lot of time, but time I had, money I didn't. Each week I would buy enough framing to keep going until the next paycheck. I spent the entire summer building it with the assistance of my two year old son Michael and a few neighbors. John, Ethel's husband, worked as a mason and offered to help me put in the cinder blocks. When ever I worked on the garage, my son Mike was right behind me getting into some kind of trouble. His mother wasn't very happy whenever he came into the house crying with a bruised knee or a splinter, but he didn't seem to care because he kept coming out for more. When that garage was finished, I was the envy of two of my neighbors who didn't buy the garage for the same reason we didn't.

Besides being a good mason, John was also an avid golfer. He had been trying to get me to learn how to play ever since I move into the development. He had an old set of golf clubs that he didn't use anymore and offered them to me, if I wanted to learn. There's a lot of open ground in the development where the future homes hadn't been built as yet, so John used it as his personal driving range. I took the clubs and started to hit golf balls when ever he had free time. We would hit every golf club in the bag until he thought I had the hang of it. I never really mastered the game, but it was a lot of fun when we finally started to play. This is how and why I ever got started playing golf.

Jo was pregnant again and due to deliver in August. When Mike was born, I rushed to the hospital and waited over six hours before the baby was born. When it came time to take her to the Lady of Lourdes Hospital for Danny, I took my time, had a shower, ate breakfast and then took her to the hospital. Dan was born one hour later at 8:27 on August 27, 1960 and weighed six pounds two and one half ounces. Boy, did I cut that close. That afternoon my good friend John's wife Ethel gave birth to her fourth daughter in the same hospital. When it was time for Jo to come home from the hospital, Ethel was also discharged so John and I drove to the hospital to pick them up together. The couple who lived two doors down from Ethel and the couple on the corner were also about to deliver at the same hospital. As I remember, that must have been a cold winter.

By the time Danny was born I had finally mastered the art of putting on a diaper without having it fall off every time you picked him up. Even though I could now put them on right, I wish we could have afforded the use of a diaper service. I would still hate changing the diapers, but at least I wouldn't have to rinse them out before putting them in a hamper. That same week I received an official looking envelope from the Department of the United States Navy. It contained my official discharge from the U.S. Navy, to be effective on July 1,1960. The truth is, I had completely forgotten about it, besides I had no intentions of re-enlisting.

Thanksgiving was coming and I had the drive to Norwich to look forward to. At least this time I had a decent car with four good tires, but I still had rte. 611 to deal with. This two lane highway always had something holding us up, it seemed as though all the state did was repair it for one reason or another, or it flooded out in the area of the Delaware Water Gape. Today, we have the Northeast Extension of the Turnpike connecting us with Rte. 81 all the way to Canada. A drive that used to take use eight to nine hours to drive, now only takes about four and a half hours. Having a six lane highway sure made the drive a pleasure. It always feels good to see the family at Thanksgiving even though it was never a big holiday in our house. But, my mother would always put with a turkey and all the trimmings. After dinner, we would sit around the table for a while bringing each other up to date, then help with the clean up and the holiday was over. When ever I was in Norwich, I always made it a point to visit with my aunts and uncles because they always made me feel wanted and were interested in what I had been doing. We would talk about just anything that came to mind, whether it was about my family or there's. There would be a lot of conversations about remember when, or did you hear about this or that. Before you knew it, three hours had passed and it was time to go, and we would look forward to visiting again the next time.

Christmas was one of the holidays that were always celebrated in Atlantic City with Jo's family. It consisted of her parents and her sister's family of seven, plus two uncles and a dozen nieces and nephews, which made for a big family gathering and a very noisy day. This was in addition to other relatives who were coming and going all day long, as the holiday should be in all families. The holiday didn't stop after dinner, it lasted well into the evening. Easter was the other holiday dinner that was always that were always celebrated at her family's house, and the gathering is always the same. I never experienced this kind of togetherness in my house as a youngster. The only family get together we had was at Thanksgiving and that included only our immediate family. I remember the Christmases my grandparents had when I was a little boy. This was the only family gathering we ever had, but once my Grandmother passed away, the holiday also faded away. This was also the year we bought our first live Christmas tree, which touched the ceiling in our living room. We've come a long way since the little fake silver tree we had in the apartment, but we still put it in the rec. room, and decorated it with the original Christmas ornaments and lights we had from the apartment. We kept that tree until it finally started to fall apart, but we still use whatever decorations were left on the big tree.

In the spring of 1962 the Warren Webster Company was sold to an investment firm and moved all of its facilities to a new location in the south. Everyone in the company was let go with the exception of some key manufacturing people and upper management. The rest of us were given a severance check and politely shown the front door. I hated leaving this job, it was close to home and a great place to work, but like so many other things, nothing lasts forever. A week later I was hired by a job shop in Philadelphia to make plant layouts for a new spandex plant that was being built in Virginia. This was not a long term project, but at least it bought me some time. I would have to be on the site of the plant in order to do this. For the first two weeks I stayed in a motel, after which I went home for a weekend and brought Jo and the boys back with me. Paula, Ethel's daughter, also came as a mother's helper. I found a cottage on Moore's Lake and we moved in, bicycles and all. I couldn't have found a better place to stay than on the lake for Jo and the boys. They were enjoying themselves while I was working but on the weekends we visited all the civil war sites and the south in general. Life was good, but like all good things, it came to an end four weeks later.

I lost no time in finding another job, only this time it wasn't jobbing, it was the Boeing/Vertol Helicopter Plant in Morton, Pennsylvania. I now had what I thought to be the perfect position for me. I was hired as a tool designer with medical insurance, a retirement plan, and all the benefits that go along with working for a company of this size. I had only been working here for a short period of time when the announcement that President John F. Kennedy had been assassinated in Dallas, Texas. Everyone was caught off guard with that announcement. I remember silence reigning for a few minutes and seeing tears in the eyes of some and stares from others. It was a weird feeling, almost like he was a member of your own family. I kept getting updates on what was happening from some of the people who had called home to get what ever information they could. I never got anything first hand about the shooting until I got home and turned on my television. I didn't realize the significance of this event, at the time, but as I look back on it, I think our country has been going down hill ever since his assassination. We had a succession of civil unrest, political bickering on a huge scale, other assassinations, and of course the Viet Nam War. It seemed like we didn't have any great leadership after that for a while. But life goes on in spite of what happens in the outside world and Washington DC.

When Mike was around five years old I taught him a couple of goofy songs I had made up. His mother wasn't very happy about them, but he thought they were neat and sang them all the time. These were the words of one on them; Gut-a-rony, Merga-troy, Alcatraz, Pukearoy-Pumpernickel, Waterloo, Leonard Sigh, Peek-a-boo. I know it sounds goofy, but you try singing it fast. Later, Danny picked the words up fast, but his mother didn't like it, I guess she had no ear for good music. Later Danny would be singing these ditties, and everyone looked at him funny, thinking he was just as crazy as his father for teaching him. Children pick things up fast when they're young and sometimes they put you in an embarrassing position. Mike and Dan used to watch the Philly games with me on television. At this particular time, one of the sponsors was the Ballantine

Beer Company that had a catchy commercial set to music that went something like this; "Heyyy, get your cold beer,Heyyyy get your cold--- Ball-an-tine beer." Mike got the words and had them down perfect. We would take him to church with us every Sunday, where he would always fuss and fidget, but on this particular Sunday he decided to sing. Everyone had just finished singing a hymn, when Mike sings out loud, "Heyyyy get your cold, Hey get your cold Ballantine beer." His Mother and I were mortified, because everyone was staring at us and laughing. I don't think I was ever as embarrassed as I was that Sunday morning. But I must admit I smiled too. It was about this time that I took him trout fishing with me for the first time. We took a ten minute ride to Mullica Hill where we fished this little stream that had just been stocked with trout. It was easy walking and not very deep here, but I wasn't going to take any chances. I tied a piece of rope around his waist and the other end to a small tree. If he were to fall, it would be in about a half inch of water. I put a worm on his hook and cast it for him. As luck would have it, he got a strike on the first cast but he was so excited I had to help him land it. That little trout was only seven inches long and Mike was afraid to touch it because of the way it was flip flopping all over the ground. After I picked it up, I finally convinced him it wouldn't bite and placed it in his hands. He still wasn't convinced and dropped it, so I picked it up and put it back into the stream. On the way home he said he wanted to go again tomorrow, that was the beginning of his love for fishing and there were hundreds of tomorrows after that.

The drive to and from work every day was becoming a real drag. It was taking me over an hour every day to go to and from work during the peak working hours. This was in addition to driving from Boeing to Temple and then home three nights a week. In 1963 we sold our home in Center City and moved into an apartment in Collingswood, while we waited for our new home in Audubon to be vacated. We were only going to be here for a short time, but Michael was five years old and ready for school. At the end of our street was the Thomas Sharp School where we registered him for kindergarten. Three months later, at Christmas time he came down with a case of the chicken-pox and was the saddest looking puppy you ever saw. I persuaded a Santa Clause at one of the stores in our shopping center to come by our apartment and pay him a visit. That evening, when the door bell rang, Santa came in with his traditional "Ho, Ho, Ho, Merry Christmas." Now, Mike became the happiest puppy you've ever seen with a case chicken-pox. I remember him having a grin that went from ear to ear, it's amazing how quickly he recovered. Both of the boys had a great time here for the short stay we had in the apartment. One thing they still talk about are the squirrels we had. There was a huge oak tree that was home to two squirrels who were always hanging around. Dan started tossing peanuts to them and eventually they became pets, so we named them Oscar and Harry. When we were ready to move to our house in Audubon he wanted to know if we could take them with us. Three months later, in March, we moved into our new home on Graisbury Avenue, without Oscar and Harry.

6-1

**Sister Barb Graduation
Pierce College - 1962**

RICHARD T BIVIANO

GULF OIL PRODUCTS

Cost Per Gallon $0.30

Mike – 17 mos

Easter - 1961

Boardwalk July '61

Petting Zoo – 1962

Moores Lake Virginia - 1962

Mike (Chicken Pox) – Santa – Dan - 1988

June - 1963

Dan – 1963

Mike 2½ yrs. The Tinker
Toy Box and this Picture are
On his Desk at Work

My Mom & the Boys

CHAPTER 7
GRAISBURY AVENUE

The house on Graisbury Avenue was a two story bungalow with lots of possibilities for expansion. The kitchen was on the small side, but large enough for all of us to sit around a table comfortably. The master bedroom was on the first floor but it had a draw back, the entrance to the back yard was through our bedroom. The dining room was small, but had a large window on the back wall, which could become the entrance to the back yard. The second floor was one very big room that ran the length of the house. There was also a finished recreation room in the basement along with a good sized utility room. When we took our first look at the property we thought it was going to be too small for the four of us, but the price was right and I felt I was handy enough to make the alterations, plus we were getting a big fenced in back yard. Taking the door from our room and putting it in the dining room would solve the one big problem. After a lot of thought, we bought the house on Graisbury Avenue. The first project I started was the replacement of the back door in our room with a window. We let the dining room stay as it was because this was to be the new baby's room until we converted the upstairs into two bedrooms. By the time the baby arrived, the bedrooms were complete.

On June 11, 1964, I graduated from Temple University, with the commencement exercise being held at the Municipal Auditorium in Philadelphia. Jo was pregnant with Joann and wanted to attend the graduation ceremony. We were a little late getting there, but with some fast walking we made it on time. I didn't like the idea, but I had to leave her to fend for herself. After the graduation exercise I asked her if she had gotten a seat. It seems she met some older women who saw her with this big belly hanging in front and made sure she had a seat and was ok. It turned out these women had sons and daughters who were graduating from the medical school as doctors. Jo told me one of the women said to her, "Honey if you were ready to deliver, you couldn't have been in a better place, there are a lot of doctors graduating today including my son." Fifteen days later, on June 26th at seven minutes after eleven in the morning, Joann was born at Lady of Lourdes Hospital in Camden, N.J. She was six pounds and five ounces, twenty-one inches long and had very little hair on her head. So that people would know that the baby was as girl, Jo scotch taped a pink ribbon on her head. It took several months before the hair grew in, but when it did you never saw a prettier baby in your life. That summer Mike received his first communion. In those days a white suit was required for the ceremony, and Jo's parents offered to buy him the suit. That was a big load off my mind, now the only thing missing was a pair of shoes. Money was tighter then ever, as usual, and I just couldn't see buying white shoes that he would probably never wear again. So I took a pair of old black shoes that he had and painted them with three coats of white enamel and added a new pair of white shoelaces. I thought I was poor when I first got married, but believe me we were really poor here but you do what you "gotta do" and then move on.

I had to put up a small retaining wall in my driveway and fill in a small piece of concrete at the very end. After this was completed I got the kids together and put their hand prints into the wet piece of concrete and dated it. Thirty plus years later, Danny took his daughter to show her his hand print. This brought the owner out who wanted to know what they were doing in his driveway. When Dan told him, he took them on a tour of our old house. Good memories never go away.

We had a very big back yard that had no trees, just grass, and Mike would bring some of his friends over to play football there. Danny liked hanging around with the older boys and would pester them to let his play. I was working in the basement when Dan comes in crying and tells me they wouldn't let him play, so I went out to see why. Mike and all the other boys said he was always off sides and didn't want to play fair. When I asked him if he was off sides, he looked up at me and said, "No," paused and asked, "What's off sides?" After it was explained, I said, "You play by the rules or you don't play." Now, everyone was happy and I went back to my project.

I never had a taste for Kool-Aid, to me it was nothing but colored water and sugar, but the kids like it and you could make a gallon of it for a nickel. When vacation time came we would take day trips to the Amish country in Pennsylvania. Jo would pack a gallon of Kool-Aid with lots of ice and some cookies along with peanut butter and jelly sandwiches. We would find a nice shady tree on a back road and have a picnic. At the end of the day, on our ride home, I would ice cream and everybody was happy. We would finish the week by adding more day trips to the to Amish country, which included the Strasbury Train Exhibit, Indian Echo Caverns, Dutch Wonderland, and Hershey Park. On our way to the Amish country in the morning, Danny was getting a little itchy in the car and kept asking "When are we going to get there Dad I'm getting thirsty?" I told him if he could be real quiet for the next half hour, I'll stop at an Amish farm for some real Amish water. He was as quiet as a church mouse after that. When I stopped at a roadside market, it had an outside drinking spout, he jumped out of the car and ran straight to the fountain, afterwards he said, "Hey Dad that was the best water I ever tasted in my whole life." We still laugh about that today.

When Danny was younger he would believe just about anything I told him, particularly the wild stories I used to make up. I had a stamp collection that I was going over one evening and he was watching me sort them by countries and asked about one of the stamps and where it came from. I showed him several different stamps, pointing out where they came from on a map I had. He had heard of Germany and France but had never heard of Upper Volta, I told him the country was in Africa, which it really was. Today this country is called Burkina. I told him the country was famous for its rice pudding made with raisons and served with whipped cream. What made them even more famous was they fought a war over it. The citizens who lived in the lower part of the country felt the upper people were very stingy because they would not allow them to have raisons and whipped cream. These poor people were eating their pudding plain and felt they deserved better. After a lot of yelling went on between them, with no success, the Lower people assembled a ragtag army and declared war. The war lasted three days with nobody getting hurt, because they never fired a shot at each other. The Upper people finally realized that a war fought over raisons and whipped cream was ridiculous, and they apologized, and they've been friendly ever since. To this day, when ever Jo makes rice pudding, Dan, Mike and Joann still ask if it was the Upper Volta pudding with raisons.

One of the family treats we could always afford was the drive-in movie. For two dollars all five of us could get in, if Mike would scrunch down in the back of our station wagon, because kids under seven got in for free, and he was eight at the time. Jo would pack the usual cakes, cookies and crackers along with the ever present Kool-Aid. We would leave the house early enough to let the kids run off some energy playing with the swings and slides before the movie started. There was even a place where you could warm a bottle of milk for Joann and had a place to change her diapers. By the time the movie was over everyone was sound asleep and one by one I would carry them from the car to their beds when we went home.

One of Mike's friends was in the Cub Scouts and he wanted to join. As soon as he turned eight we went to one of the meetings and signed him up. He stayed in the cub scouts until he was twelve and moved on to the boy scouts. The old Cub Master was leaving to follow his son into the boy scouts and I took his place as the new Cub Master.

The time spent in cub scouting was an enjoyable time for both Jo and I because of all the friends we were to make, some of whom we are still very close to today. Two of them, Jim and Dorothy, who were parents of two boys in our cub pack, become two of our closest friends. My time as Cub Master ended when Danny turned twelve and went into the boy scouts program. All of the boys turned out to be good citizens and I have two of them living on my street today with families of their own. It's nice when some of the others come up and say "Hey Mr. B, you remember me?" After leaving cub scouts I went with Dan into the boy scout troop that Mike was in. Mike took scouting very serious, as he did everything, ending up an Eagle Scout before he was sixteen years old. Dan, on the other hand was a fair weather scout who only went camping in warm weather, or he didn't have anything else to do. He eventually made tenderfoot his highest rank. The first time he went to scout camp, his Mother packed his bag with clean underwear, sox, T shirts and an extra pair of pants. When we went to pick him and Mike up a week later he was still wearing the same cloths he had when he left. When we got home Jo emptied his duffle bag and found all of the clean cloths she had neatly folded lay in the bottom of his bag.

1968 was the first year since we were married that Jo and I were able to go on a vacation by ourselves. We had planned and saved for over a year, and went through dozens of brochures before picking Puerto Rico for our vacation. The boys went to a summer camp with their cousins Bob and Michael, while Joann stayed with my Mother in Law. After being on vacation for three days, Jo commented she missed them and wanted to call them. I missed them too, but not enough to call. This was the first time we were alone, and I wasn't about to spoil the great time we were having. The week went by fast, and before we knew it, it was Sunday and time to board the airplane that would take us home. By the end of the week I started to miss them as much as she did.

The following year we gave Joann a two wheel bike for her birthday, and fitted it with training wheels to make it easier for her to learn to ride. On a very hot and humid afternoon with the temperature in the 90s and 100 per cent humidity, she wanted to try to ride without the training wheels. I took them off and trotted next to her, holding her and the handle bar at the same time. Sweat was running down my face like it was coming out of a faucet, I was gasping for air and breathing so hard it's a wonder I didn't have a heart attack right then and there. She didn't solo that day, but a few days later when I wasn't home, she gets on her bike and rides with no one holding on to her, I wasn't there to see it. Isn't that the way it always turns out?

This was also the year of the Apollo flight where Neil Armstrong set foot on the moon, and a little later followed by Buzz Alden. Jo and I sat up until the wee hours of the morning to watch him gingerly stepping down a ladder and taking that first step on the moon. I also remember being cross-eyed the next morning for staying up all night, but it was worth the loss of sleep. When I went to work the next morning, it was the major topic of conversation. I guess I wasn't the only one to lose some sleep. Jo started a family tradition with birthdays that still goes on today. On everyone's birthday they can choose whatever they wanted for dinner that night including the cake. Mike was the first one to get to choose and he chooses cheeseburgers, French fries and a milk shake at McDonalds. That's not what we had in mind, but it was his choice. We went to McDonalds to have our burgers and fries, and then home, where we sang happy birthday before cutting and eating the chocolate mayonnaise cake his mother had baked for him. As the years passed so did his tastes, later he always chose any pasta dish as long as it had Moms' sauce with meatballs. His birthday cake favorite now is strawberry trifle that she makes for him every year. When it comes Danny's time he chooses pizza and soda with chocolate mayonnaise cake and ice cream on top. Jo bakes the cake and I pick up the pizza. I can't remember him ever having anything else until many years later. Joann on the other hand is different, in the beginning she wanted burgers, French fries and chocolate mayonnaise cake. But as she grew older, and depending on what diet she was on, it was always changing. Years later she chose a sit down dinner at a nice restaurant, ordering something expensive with all the trimmings, and any cake, as long as it had pink icing and she wasn't paying for it. Believe it or not this tradition is still carried on.

After seven years of what I thought was a secure position with the company I was laid off, along with over 9,000 other people. We had a good product but, a small market for military helicopters. With the situation in Viet Nam and the fall of Saigon, there were very few military contracts. I was again able to find a position job shopping, but this time I told myself this was the last time. One of my old job shops heard from someone they had just hired that I was looking for work and called me. They had a short time position with a company in Philadelphia for someone to do board work. The Boeing layoff saturated the job market with draftsmen, designers and engineers, making it difficult to find a new position. I didn't particularly want to go back to job shopping, but I needed the work. After spending over two years of the so called "short time assignment," I decided it was time to look for a new position with benefits, a future and a retirement plan. Job shopping was never a secure position with any of the companies it represented, however it paid well, but offered no security, few benefits and no retirement. After seventeen years in the engineering field, I felt it was time to change. I began looking for a new position with the benefits I was looking for. The Allstate Insurance Company was expanding its sales force, and I thought if my friend Jim could do this, I knew I could. I never mentioned to him that I had put in an application, but when I did, he said "It's the best decision you ever made" and as it turned out, it was. The company sent me to their insurance school for two weeks to prep me for the state exams. I took the tests, passed them, and the next thing I knew I was standing behind a booth in a Sears stores soliciting business. This one decision changed my life more than anything else I had done in the past. At thirty-nine years old I had everything I wanted, stability, fringe benefits, and a retirement and profit sharing plan. Except for the little training I had at the school, I knew from nothing about insurance or sales, but I bluffed my way in the door, and told them in so many words I was the greatest thing since sliced bread, I was that confident of succeeding. The first thing I did was to tag cars in the Patco High Speed Line Parking lot. Jo, Mike and Danny chipped in by making sure that every car in the lot had a brochure on its windshield. That night when I got home I received a phone call from the parking lot attendant who was mildly upset with me, because most of the brochures on the cars ended up on the parking lot macadam and he had to pick them up. Oh well, so much for tagging cars. I really worked hard that year, doing everything I was taught at school. Tagging cars, mass mailings, handed out fliers and X-dated everyone I talked to. This effort and my standing behind the traditional Allstate booth at Sears got me going. I started as an agent officially in September of 1972, on the eve of the state mandated insurance program, or as it was to be known "No Fault Insurance." The backbone for any successful salesman is the "X-date" and boy did I have X-dates for January, 1973. Since I was the new agent, I had the late store hours on New Years Eve. I will never forget that evening, as I was standing at my car in the Sears parking lot with the trunk of my car open. After the store closed this was my office so to speak, where I wrote nine auto policies to be effective January first at midnight. Seven of these were in the State Assigned Risk Program and the other two were written directly with Allstate. I was on my way and never looked back. At the end of my first full year I made the company conference of champions award and a trip to San Juan Puerto Rico with Jo for six days, and all expenses paid. I was on cloud nine and it never stopped until I retired twenty-one years later. Life was really good, working for Allstate gave me the freedom I never had for my family. I can't remember ever missing anything the kids did at or after school. I was able to go to Little League Baseball, High School football, plays, piano recitals and all the other programs the kids were involved in. What more could I have asked for?

The boys were in the Boys Scout and JoAnn wanted to be part of something and wanted to join the Girl Scouts. She had only been in Brownies for a short time when there was a Father/Daughter Valentine Dance and of course I went. It was kind of weird seeing grown men dancing with these little spindly legged eight and nine year old girls. It may have been a little awkward, but the truth be known we all loved it, besides, that's what it's all about. She was so proud to have me there I thought she was going to bust. A short time after this she asked me to go to her piano recital. She had been taking piano lessons since she was five and I had been listening to her every time she was practicing at home. But this was different, this was a command performance I could never say no to. I can honestly say that it was the longest hour and a half I've ever spent sitting on a chair. As terrible as most of the playing was, Joann was by far the best sounding one there, or maybe I might have been a little prejudice. A few weeks after the recital, it was Girl Scout cookie time. I hate to tell you how many boxes of cookies I bought, but P. T. Barnum had me in mind when he said, "There's one born every day."

When Mike was sixteen he reached the rank of Eagle Scout and was awarded his badge at an awards banquet. After the awards ceremony Jim and Dorothy came over to our house for coffee and we started talking about the kids when they were young. I was telling them about something that occurred a few years back. One night after dinner Jo informed me that something was broken and no one would own up to who was responsible. I started with Mike, "Did you do it?" Mike says "No", "Dan "did you do it?" Dan says "No". Every time I asked Joann anything she would start sniffling whether she was guilty or not, and she says no. I looked at Jo, smiled and said, "The L Bs" must have done it again." Everyone looked at me, including Jo who had a frown on he face and asked "What are L. Bs.?." I said, "Late at night when everyone is sound asleep, these "Little Bastards" (L.Bs.) would come out of the woodwork and either break or hide what was broken or missing." Jim roared with laughter when he heard the ending and said that was the best story he had ever heard and wished he had thought of it first. The four of us had been going to the Poconos every January for the past few years. We called these getaways our annual getting away from everything, including the kids time. All of the weekends were memorable for one reason or another, but I must tell you about this one in particular. We had decided to try one of the honeymoon lodges with the heart shaped tub, bed, sinks and lounges. I don't remember if the toilet was heart shaped or not, but with the red rugs and mirrors we felt like we were in a French bordello. The four of us got together in one of the rooms and laughed at what we saw for over half an hour before leaving for dinner. But the biggest laugh was to come after dinner in the lounge. We had been tobogganing in the afternoon and didn't bother to change our clothes for dinner. After dinner we went to see the show in the lounge with one of the acts being a belly dancer. After she finished her routine she asked for two volunteers to come up on the stage. Let me explain that I am not an exhibitionist, and I do not like to be singled out. Jim on the other hand, lives for these moments and volunteered not only him but, me as well. I was trying to wiggle out of this but got goaded into it by not only the audience but my own wife and Dorothy. The dancer made us roll up our pant legs which showed our long johns and high top boots. She then put a cape on both of us which made us look like two supermen. After showing us a few of her movements she had us dance along with her, and boy did we look ridiculous. Everybody had a good laugh out of this and as embarrassed as I was, I went along with the crowd. After the dance she asked where we were from and what we did for a living, of course Jim had to tell her where he was from and who he worked for. She asked me the same questions, but my answers were all together different. I want you to know when you tell a lie you have to continue to tell more lies to make the story believable. I told her I wasn't from Audubon, but just visiting Jim for the week. She asked where I was from, now the lies become bigger and bigger. I said I was from Broken River, Montana, a place I didn't know exited. Then she asked what I did for a living, and I told her I ran a sheep ranch. Then it was more questions and now more lies. The more she asked, the deeper in trouble I got. Jim, Dorothy and Jo were laughing themselves silly while I was dying up there. I was one happy camper when it was over. As we were walking out of the lounge a familiar looking woman came up to me and said, "You're not from Montana, you're my insurance agent!" I was so embarrassed I wanted to crawl under a rock and die. For the next fifteen years when ever she or her husband came to see me in my office, they would always remind me of that night and asks me if I was still belly dancing.

"Man and His World" was the destination for the family vacation in 1976. Instead of driving directly to Montreal we went up the Western part of New England through Connecticut, Massachusetts and Vermont. This gave the kids a chance to see a different part of the country. Our first big stop was Brattleboro, Vermont, where we spent the night in a motel. The kids loved this place because they had a big swimming pool and we let them stay there until it was time to go to bed. After breakfast the next morning for the top of the Green Mountains. We made a stop at one of the overlooks to see the view, but the only thing the kids wanted to see is was a place for lunch. After lunch we headed we headed for Middleboro where we had dinner and spent the night at a motel that had a pool for the kids to play in for a while. The next morning we went to see the Morgan Horse Farm. After seeing the horse farm we drove directly to Montreal where we stayed at the Bonaventure Hotel. "Man and His World," was the originally site of the 1967 World's Fair. It seemed like every country in the world had a pavilion here, and we visited every one of them. After three days of walking around the park, we had had it with "Man and His World." But, before we left we visited the Loenbrough Brewing Tent. Even though Mike wasn't quite old enough drink beer, I treated him to his first and only legal beer."

The next morning we headed for home making stops in New England to see some more of the sights. A great time was had by all that year, but it would be the last time the five of us would go on vacation together as a family for a very long time.

I had been taking Dan and Mike fishing with me ever since they were big enough to hold a pole. We had been watching all of the fishing shows that were on television every Saturday morning for several years. When we were not watching the TV, we were discussing the possibility of going on one of these trips. I discussed this possibility with Jo, who was not at all that crazy about the idea, but reluctantly gave her approval. The discussion became a reality when I located a cabin with a boat and motor on the St Lawrence River and rented it for one week. I don't know who was more excited about the trip, me or the boys, because that's all we talked about that entire spring until we left in June. The last thing Jo said to me before we left was, "If you don't bring both of them home, don't come back." You might have thought we were going on a safari in the Belgium Congo instead of a cabin on the St. Lawrence River in New York State. Once we loaded up the car and backed it out of the driveway it seemed to take forever to get there. The drive only took about seven hours, but it seemed to take twice that much time because we were in a big hurry to get there.

Every morning the boys were up before sunrise and ready to go. I wasn't too happy about getting up before daylight, but the best fishing is supposed to be at sunrise. I never saw them eat a bowl of cereal as fast as they did that first morning, they were just frothing at the bit to go. I could never think of a word better then "excited" to describe how they were that week. If they had their way we would have left the cabin at daybreak every morning and not return until nightfall, but I had no intentions of doing that. We would leave early in the morning and be back by noon for lunch and then go back until it was time for dinner. This was alright for the first two days but after that I needed a little nap in the afternoon. I told them they could fish off the dock and along the shore in front of the cabin and to keep a few fish for tonight's dinner. When I got up they handed me a pail full of small fish that took me over an hour to clean and fillet. As promised, I dipped them in pancake batter and deep fried the entire pail of fish. We had so many fillets that it took three trips back and forth to the deep fry to cook them while they ate them faster then I could put them on the table. After dinner I told them not to keep fish unless they were at least fourteen inches long. The next afternoon instead of a nap, I taught them how to fillet fish. We had a lot of laughs and a lot of fun that week, but before we knew it, the week was up and we had to pack for the trip home. It turned out to be one of the most memorable and enjoyable time I've ever spent with them. I was probably never as close to the boys as I was that week. After returning home, we were all sitting around the dinner table talking about the adventures we had, when I said to Jo she might like to come along next year. At that point Danny quickly jumped up and said, "No Dad, she'll spoil everything and make wash all the time." To this day, I don't think he has ever changed his way of thinking, or of thinking what he says. This trip was to last for the next thirty-seven years without a miss and is still going strong in 2010. Even though Dan missed a few years for one reason or another, Mike has been on every trip. He has kept a diary with the number of fish caught, lures used, and the weather conditions ever since the first trip to the St. Lawrence when we tacked a brown paper bag on the wall of our cabin and made a chart of what we caught each day.

Living in the house on Graisbury Avenue was a real treat for me. We may have had some hard times in the beginning, but I felt that we got more enjoyment out of what we did together as a family. Watching and taking part in the growing up of the boys and Joann, was something very special. There were times when they made me angry about messy rooms, homework, chores and all the other things that growing children do. A good example of anger is when they're doing something they know they shouldn't be doing, but are doing it anyway. A neighbor wanted to give them some guppies to put in fish bowl, I wasn't crazy about the idea but I said ok. This ended up with a five gallon tank full of guppies, gold fish and some other assorted fish. The bottom of the tank was covered with small stones and clay ornaments. One night they were playing with the tank and somehow it landed on the rec. room floor with a big bang. When I got there, the floor was covered with broken glass, water, stones and flopping fish all over the place, and I was angry to say the least. Today when that story comes up, everybody laughs, including me. However, there were a lot more memories with smiles and laughs, than there were over the fish tank fiasco.

By now the kids were getting bigger and the house was getting smaller. We had finally outgrown the house on Graisbury Avenue. We could see this coming, Mike was seventeen and would be starting his senior year in September and graduating in June 1976. Danny would be starting his sophomore year and Joann was going into junior high. She always had her own room, while Dan and Mike shared one and I felt they should all have their own rooms as well. We wanted to stay in Audubon and started looking for a little bigger house. We found the house we wanted the following spring, but it would need some alterations to make it the way we wanted. We put our bid in, and after a little finagling over the cost we signed an agreement of sale in April and made settlement in August of 1977.

Earlier this year I was summoned to sit on a New Jersey Grand July. I had been called for jury duty once before but the trial I was supposed to sit was called off and I was sent home. A Grand Jury is completely different then the run of the mill jury trial, in that you do not rule a decision of guilty or not guilty. You sit in a court room without a judge and listen to one side of a prosecutor's case. Your job is to help rule that there is enough evidence to proceed with a trial. During the course of twenty-six weeks you will probably hear several witnesses and listen to phone taps all day long. You might hear witnesses in four unrelated cases one week and the next week one case. We were allowed to take notes on what we heard each week so that we can continue to deal with each case as they come up. At the end of each session the note books were kept until we meet again. In the beginning I became bored with just listening to people talk, but as the weeks dragged on I found myself looking forward to the next sitting to hear more about a particular case. The cases I heard were primarily fraud and illegal gambling, but I did hear information on two murder cases as well. Even though I couldn't rule on the outcome of the cases I heard, I found this to be a great experience. When I was first notified of the grand Jury, I had some people tell me to find a reason to get of going. I'm glad I didn't listen to them because it was a great experience and one I shall never forget.

After several trips to various colleges in New Jersey Mike decided on Ramapo College. When it came time him to leave for school we loaded up the car with everything from his stereo to the clothes he would be wearing. If that wasn't enough, his Mother had to make sure he had enough to eat for the next month. When we finally left, there was just enough room for him to sit in the back seat along with everything else we couldn't fit in the trunk. I hate to think of what it would have been like if we had a compact car. I remember the scene when we were ready to go home, his Mother cried for the next two days because she missed him already. I kept telling her he was only ninety miles from home and not in some god forsaken foreign land. Two weeks later I was forced to take her to Ramapo to show her he was ok. When we got to the apartment in the dorm that he was sharing with two other boys, I thought she was going to feint. The sink was full of dirty dishes and a pile of dirty laundry was tossed in the corner of his bedroom. Like so many woman, she couldn't stand to see a "little mess." The first thing she did was wash the dishes then fixed the bed and put all of his dirty laundry in a pillow case to take home to be washed. I think she overacted, because I would have left the mess the way it was and let them clean it up. After that visit, I can't remember going to Ramapo again for the rest of the year. Mike was coming home pretty regular after that and bringing his dirty laundry with him. We had put money in his budget to cover getting his clothes cleaned at school and not at home. But Jo would say she didn't mind doing it. Maybe she didn't care, but I did.

I remember a quote that I read in a magazine that said, "It's never too late to have a happy childhood, but the second one is up to you and nobody else." I think Graisbury Avenue was my second one because I was living it through the eyes of my children.

I wish I had a way of attaching the 8mm video I made for my wife as a twenty fifth anniversary present to this journal . It contains so many things that I can not put into words and pictures. When I think back to the early years when the kids were young, I miss hearing them yell when they were young, "Daddy's home".

The President and Board of Trustees of
Temple University
request the honor of your presence at the
Seventy-eighth Annual Commencement
Thursday morning, June eleventh
Nineteen hundred and sixty-four
at ten thirty o'clock
Municipal Auditorium
Thirty-fourth Street below Spruce
Philadelphia, Pennsylvania

Paul and Barbara
Joann Christening

Joann – 3 mos.

Mike Communion – 1965

Paul Wedding – 1969

Bowman Lake Picnic

Eagle Scout Ceremony – 1974

Joann Communion – 1972

Joann Solos on Her Bike 1970

7-3

Before the Bedroom Door became a window

Sally Star & Joann

Mike – 1963

Dan – 1965

Joann – 1969

KINDERGARTEN

Heart Shaped Bathtub - Poconos

Dan – Mike – Joann 1975

31 th. Birthday

Upper Volta Stamps

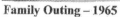

Family Outing – 1965

Mike 1967

Cub Scout Outing – 1971

CHAPTER 8
PARK PLACE

This was the third and probably the last home we would ever buy. It took a few years to make all the changes we wanted before we could say this was the perfect house. When we were finally finished, it had five bedrooms, a big living room, a dining room, a recreation room with a huge fireplace, a kitchen with dinner area and a barbeque pit. This pit was a big hit with the kids when we moved in. They liked cooking their own hotdogs and marsh mellows on long barbeque forks I had bought for them. We all had a lot of fun with this over the years I even liked doing my hot dogs.

While Mike was in school we curtained off a big space of the basement with a bed, a night table and a lamp where he would sleep whenever he came home. We had to do this because the contractors were ready to add the addition for the two new bedrooms. When he came home for the first time he was a little surprised to find he was sleeping in the basement. He would get his old bedroom back when the builders were finished and Joann and Danny moved into the new rooms.

The first four years in our first house in Mantua, plus the fourteen years on Graisbury Ave., were the years we as parents were raising babies and young children. Moving into Park Place was something entirely different, here we were raising teenagers. When they were babies we had to feed and care for them, later when they started walking and talking we had to teach and show them right from wrong, behavior, responsibility and what the word "No" means. You can't be friends with your children at that age because you are a teacher, but what you can do is give them all the love you have. Doctor Phil may disagree with me about being friends, but I strongly believe it this. Teenagers on the other hand are harder to teach and can not be treated as little children. They are passing into adulthood and think they have all the answers and we as adults know they don't. But as time goes by they begin to realize how wise we were and how sorry they were for not listening to what we had to say. Dan was probably the biggest breaker of the rules. He thought they were meant for everyone but him. One of the first memories I have of Danny in the new house was his coming home late for dinner one night. We had just finished eating dinner and he hadn't come home as yet. It was getting dark and we started to wonder where he could be, when he pops in by the side door all excited about something and carrying a bundle wrapped in newspaper under his arm. He had caught a big bass and stopped at the local deli to get it weighted on their scale. At that moment I asked why he didn't call to tell us where he was. He gave his usual answer, "I forgot," and proceeded to tell me about the fish he had caught. The Deli owner told him it weighted seven pounds and eleven ounces. The deli owner called the Camden Courier-Post about the fish he had caught, and the following day a small article appeared in the paper. I was angry at him for not calling us, but I congratulated him on the big fish and then scolded him about what he had done and reminded him he had to be more responsible or he would be losing his privileges the next time. Several months later Dan had to learn the hard way by not listening. He had been pestering me to get him a moped for his birthday, but I told him they were dangerous and I didn't think it was a good idea. He had a friend who had one of these and couldn't understand why I was against him having one. I tried to explain that all kinds of bad things can happen on these bikes, but I was thinking like as an adult and not a teenager. When he said he wanted to buy one with his own money, I told him if he did, I'd just run over it with the car the first time I saw it in the driveway and he would not only lose the bike, but the money he spent to buy it. On a Saturday morning in October I received a phone call from a friend who called to tell me that Dan had just been hit by a car in front of his house. I stopped what I was doing and raced over to the scene of the accident to see what happened. I arrived just in time to see the ambulance getting ready to take him to the hospital, so I jumped in and went with him. The Medics were working on him all the way to the hospital, he was unconscious and he had a nasty gash on the side of his head which made me very nervous. At the hospital I waited for him to come too, but the doctors told me to go home and they would call when they had some answers. Now I had to face his Mother and tell her what happened. When I came in she was making dinner and I didn't know what to say, so I waited until I worked up the nerve to tell her. He had borrowed his friend's moped and had taken it for a ride. I was told he came out of a side street without looking and was struck by a car. When I finished telling her, everything I knew, we went straight to the hospital. When I left him to come home he was in the emergency room, but when we got to the hospital we were told he was now in intensive care. When we saw him for the first time in intensive care we were both scared. He didn't look good and he hadn't gained consciousness yet, and the fear of losing him took hold of both of us. About an hour later he moved and spoke, but we couldn't understand what he was saying. When the doctor finally came in, he explained what was wrong and what they were going to do. He had a concussion, a broken femur bone in his left leg and contusions and bruises all over his body. They couldn't give him much for his pain because of the head wound, but when that was taken care of they would set his leg. We were told a metal rod would be inserted into the leg to replace the broken and shattered femur bone. Once this was done he remained in the hospital for eight days. When we brought him home he was laid up for about six weeks. The school made arrangements for him to have a tutor at home so he could keep up with his school work. One night some of his friends came over and wanted to take him out for a pizza, and I said I didn't think that was a good idea. Because of the static I was getting from everybody, including his Mother, against my better judgment I said yes, but I wanted him home in one hour and not a minute later. A half hour later they came home and I knew something was wrong. On the ride over to the pizza parlor they were in an accident. Someone had hit them on the passenger side of the car, where Dan was sitting. He wasn't hurt and the boys were not to blame, but they were scared. I was angry at myself for letting him go, but after this, Hell would freeze over before I give in to them again. In June Dan graduated from high school, but had no desire to continue schooling to learn a trade or profession. I explained to him that he had to have some plan for the future on how he would make a living. He wasn't interested in the future, he just wanted to take life easy. He did have two years of machine shop in high school and used this experience to get a job as an apprentice in a tool and die shop. He stayed there for about a year, and decided he wanted to visit my sister Barb and her husband on their ranch in Colorado. He stayed with them for three weeks, and headed for some friends in California, where he found a job and stayed for the next two years.

In March of 1978 I gave Jo a toy poodle for her birthday. He weighed around three pounds and was no longer than a can of beans. We had him registered with the American Kennel Club under the name of Brutus Maximillan Biviano. With a name like you would think he was a fighter but he wasn't, he was afraid of his own shadow. Jo and the kids just loved him because he was so small and fragile. One night we had friends over for the evening and one of them owned two wolf hounds. When he saw the dog and heard what we had named him laughed out loud. I said, "You better watch what you say, he knows karate." When I looked over to Brutus I said, "Attack" and he walked over to Ray and licked his hand. This made Ray and everybody else laugh even more. We all had a lot of fun with him for the next two years until he was killed by our neighbors' dog. When you are attached to a pet like him you feel like you've lost a close friend and you morn. It took a long time to get over his death, particularly for Jo because it was her dog.

Mike and now Dan have flown the coop leaving us with just one chick left, Joann. I spent a lot of time with the boys watching ballgames, fishing, and camping when they were younger and I missed them not being home anymore. I always looked at Joann as the baby, but now I see her growing up as a teenager and a pretty young lady. I would get angry at the boys when they goofed off or did something stupid, but I could never really get angry at her because she acted so coy with me when I had to correct her. She made me laugh at some of the reasons she had for doing things or looking at me like a sick puppy. I was mowing the lawn one day when I noticed a pile of cigarette butts next to the house. I was trying to figure out how they had gotten there, when I glanced up and saw the window in Joann's room. When I confronted her she said they were not her cigarettes. I should have known better, in theory they may not have been her cigarettes because she bummed them from her friend. Instead of asking her if they were hers, I should have asked if she smoked them, then she wouldn't have been as evasive, as she was trying to be. I said "I guess someone was walking along the street one day and said, I think I'll throw this ash tray full of cigarettes butts under Joann's window." She looked at me and laughed at my little story, but she knew I had her dead to rights. If she smoked after this, I never saw her, but I never knew for sure. At one time or another, I made it very clear I didn't want any of the kids to smoke while they were in school, or at any other time. After they graduated and were on their own, I told them, if they wanted to, it was up to them, but I didn't recommend it. Mike and Dan still smoke today, but JoAnn doesn't and neither does her son Alex.

We didn't see much of the boys, Dan was in California with his friends and Mike was in his second year at Ramapo. However, he did come home once a month, but I think it was only to get his laundry done and have his mother load him up with food to take back. No mater how much fuss I made over him bringing his laundry home, she said she didn't mind. The thing is I minded, but deep down I also missed him and enjoyed it when he came home, laundry and all, but I had to "Bark," because that's what fathers do. When he came home for summer brake he hit us with a bomb shell at dinner time saying he was not going back to school in the fall. We were not expecting this, and it caught both of us completely off guard. When I finally caught my breath I said, "Why?" He said, "I'm going to backpack and work my way across Europe with John and stay in hostels at night." I'm going to relate to you the conversation we had as close as I can remember that night. Dad in a very calm voice asked, "How are you going to pay for this trip?" Mike answers, "I'll save the money I earn this summer and use this." Dad, again in a very calm voice asked, "How are you going to save money for your trip when you start paying board tomorrow and a big car insurance bill due in August?" Mike, "But Dad ---," at this point Dad interferes because Dad can interfere when he wants to. Dad in a much sterner voice says, "You hear me out, if you don't go back to school in the fall, I won't be angry because it's your life and your decision. But remember the talk we had before you left for school, there were no second chances if you flunk out or quit." I knew I was putting a lot of pressure on him, but he had to understand how important this decision was. I said to him, "You can live at home, but you will have to pay his your own way and keep respectable hours. If you want to hitch hike your way across Europe and live in hostels, go ahead because I will not stop you. But I can tell you one thing, you'll enjoy that trip a thousand times over if you stay in a nice hotel and have a rented car instead of hitchhiking and sleeping in hostel. If it were me, I'd opt for the hotel and car." Mike never did go back to school, but he found a job in sales and stuck to it for several years. Today he and his partner Alan are owners of a good sized construction company and when he and his wife go on vacation, they always stay at a nice hotel with a rented car. I guess he remembered my words of wisdom from way back when.

By now I had been with Allstate for five years and during that time I had won two company conference trips to Puerto Rico and Hawaii as well as a few other weekends to places that were warm in the winter. We were developing the travel bug for the winter season and warm beaches, and decided to go to Acapulco where it was warm. On the beach at our hotel they had parasailing rides that took you over and around Acapulco Bay that sounded like a lot of fun. There was a long line of people waiting to make the trip, but for me it was worth the wait. My turn finally came and after a briefing of what to do and what to expect I was ready to go. The ride lasted about fifteen minutes but I could have stayed up for an hour that's how much I enjoyed the view, the ride and the experience of floating in air. After I came down I told Jo that she should try this because I thought she would really enjoy it as much as I did, but she said, "No." Some of the other girls who had already taken the ride, convinced her she was missing out on something very special, and then she said yes. While she was airborne I was taking pictures of her in various stages of the ride. When she finally came down I was excited for her and said, "Wasn't that the greatest sight you've ever seen?" She looked at me and said, "I don't know, I had my eyes closed the entire time!," I couldn't believe she said that. Four weeks later her picture was on the front page of the travel section of a Philadelphia, newspaper touting Mexico as a vacation spot. There must have been someone from the newspaper on the beach that day writing a featured story on Acapulco and snapped the picture of her floating down in her parachute just as she was ready to land. I still have the newspaper clippings and the front page picture.

When Dan finally came home from California, he arrived on the seat of a Harley-Davidson Motorcycle of all things. I guess he forgot about he the moped accident. He needed a job for the summer so he called the owner of the cabins we had rented on the St. Lawrence and ask if they were hiring. They said they needed someone to run the bait shop for them in the morning. If he wanted the job he could stay in the back rooms which had a small kitchen and a room with a bed and television in it. When Mike and I went fishing there that year, he joined us on occasions, when he wasn't working, for a visit or to have dinner with us. You didn't have to see him coming, you could hear him coming with that gutted muffler he had on that cycle. The highway was half a mile away and you could hear the echo of that muffler every time he came and left. Mike and I would laugh every time we heard it and wondered why he was never stopped by a state trooper. Even though he didn't go fishing with us, it was nice to have him with us again. One morning we were fishing in an area called Goose Bay when a rapala lure was driven deep into the meaty part of my hand. We went to the local hospital and had a doctor take it out. When he was finished he handed my lure back to me in a specimen jar. When I asked him why the jar, he explained. A few years ago someone like me came in with the same problem. When it was taken out he gave the man back his lure and he left. A few minutes later he came back. He had put the lure in his hand and was opening the car door with that hand. He drove one of the hooks back into his hand, next to where he had just had it taken out. Ever since then he gives the lure back to them in a specimen jar. When he told us this, we thought it was a joke, but he said it wasn't a joke, its' was a true story.

Being a loyal Philadelphia Eagle fan who had been suffering and frustrated since 1975 with a team that was losing year after year we finally had a decent team. This year they made it to the Super Bowl for the first time. After watching the game on television with high hopes I was again disappointed, they lost 27-10. As the years passed I've forgotten about the loss, but I have one funny memory that will never be forgotten. The weather for the playoff game that put the Eagles in the Super Bowl, in December, with the Dallas Cowboys was as brutal as it comes. This was the kind of weather the Eskimos live for. The wind was howling, the temperature was in the low 20s and to make it even colder we were sitting in front of the entrance that brought us to our seats in the 700 level. Sitting in front of the entrance steps was like being in front of a wind tunnel. As cold as it was, I'm going to relate a scene of what it was like in our seats that day. For the past couple of years at Christmas time the boys and I were buying Jo clothes to wear that would make her warmer and more comfortable, particularly for this playoff game. She was wearing thermal long johns covered with a sweat suit, a hooded sweater and toped off with an old alpaca coat. By now you have that picture in your mind. In addition to the clothes she was wearing, she had on a pair of gloves that were heated by batteries, as well as her ear muffs, and a pair of stockings. It waS all she could do to walk to the stadium from the car. She had so much clothing on she was walking like a mummy. In addition to the clothes, she wanted me to bring my portable TV, with a five inch screen, to put on her lap. Once she was comfortable she pulled a blanket over her head and watched the game on TV. Except for some hot chocolate now and then, she never took her head out until it was time to go home. She was the talk of the 700 level for the entire game. While everyone was laughing, I must admit I was laughing also because she was probably the smartest and warmest person in the stadium that day.

1981 may not have been what I wanted for the Eagles, but it sure was for Joann. First it was the Junior Prom which showed her for what she was, a beautiful young lady all dressed up for the first time in a formal gown to attend her Junior Prom. In November she was a nominee for Home Coming Queen and two weeks later a contestant in the New Jersey Junior Miss Pageant. She, along with another girl from a different community were sitting in the rumble seat of a two door vintage Ford, waving, smiling and eating up all the attention they were getting while being paraded around the area in a train of convertibles and vintage cars. The parade ended at the civic center where the contestants were getting ready to go on stage for the talent contest and later they would be paraded in their gowns. Joann played a snappy Scott Joplin number on the piano that everyone seemed to enjoy, by the sound of the ovation they gave. When the formal time came, she was escorted to the stage, dressed in a pink gown, holding the arm of her military escort. She may not have been selected Junior Miss when it was all over, but having the poise and nerve to go through with this, made her mother and father so very proud of her. Joann had had been taking piano lessons since she was six years old. I remember the early years when she was practicing her lessons how terrible they sounded. But as the years passed she was getting better and by the time she was a teenager she was a pleasure to listen to. By the time she was a senior in high school, her Mother and I thought she might want to continue into a musical career. We were very surprised when she said she wanted to study fashion design. We were a little disappointed but it was her choice and after graduating the following June, she entered school in the fall for fashion design only to come home after the first semester and telling her Mother she change her mind and wanted her to break the news to me. Jo tells me she's supposed to soften me up because Joann thinks I'm going to get mad and holler at her because about quitting. When I finally got to sit down and talk to her, I asked why she wanted to leave, but before I finished my question she starts to sniffle, and then answers, "You said we all get one chance to go to school and I've used up mine," all the while sniffling as she tells me this. I hate it when she puts on the tear bags, it makes me feel bad, but this time I had to laugh because it was so phony. I asked her if she had another plan in mind. She says she wants to go to an Executive Secretarial School that she had already looked into. I said it was a long way from fashion design, but if you really want this, I have no objection. She graduated with honors and found a job with a big law firm. We established ten dollars a week as her board, which was like saying you can stay home for free. She gives the board money to her Mother, not knowing we had opened a savings account with her money. A few weeks later she tells her Mother she can't pay her board this week for some forgotten reason. So Mom lets her slide, and again several weeks later she does the same thing only this time it's for a different reason. Jo keeps me informed, but Joann doesn't know what I know. One night after dinner she says she and her cousin Donna were discussing getting an apartment and what did I think about the idea. I said, "Why don't you do it?" She wasn't expecting that for an answer from me, but she answers with words to this effect, not realizing she answered her own question, "Do you realize I have car payments, gas and lunch money every week, not to mention my board money. Then there's my car insurance, which leaves me with nothing left at the end of the week, besides, I can't even afford to live home, let alone an apartment." I said to her, while laughing, "Honey, you better get used to that, because that's what life is all about in the real world. You can have what you can afford." The subject never came up again.

Hula Dancers

Me and Two Agents – 1975
Conference of Champions

Jo on the Beach at Waikiki

Belly Dancing – Poconos

Summit – Poconos – 1974

Dan – 1976
7 lbs.-11ozs.

Jo Para Sailing – Acapulco

Lake Nasignon

Dan and His Cycle 1980

The Bull Never Wins in Spain

Super Bowl – 1981

Jr Miss Pageant 1981

Isle of Capri 1982

25th. Wedding Anniversary

Tangiers 1980

CHAPTER 9
HONG KONG & THE ORIENT

I have no idea how Hong Kong, China, Thailand or the Philippines look today, but I do remembered vividly what they looked like in 1981 when Jo and I celebrated our twenty-fifth wedding anniversary. If we were looking for something different to do, this was it. We boarded a Korean Airline jet at JFK International, bound for Anchorage, Alaska. This would complete the first leg of our flight to China. After arriving in Anchorage we had a crew change and then we took off on the second leg of our journey to Seoul, Korea. By this time we were saddle sore from sitting on an airplane for over sixteen hours, but we knew we were getting close. After a short stay, and another crew change we were on our way to the Kai Tak Airport in Hong Kong. We had gone through two crew changes, eleven time zones and twenty-three hours of waiting and flying, with a few short cat naps thrown in before finally landing in Hong Kong. As beat and tired as we were, we forgot about it on our bus ride from the the airport to our hotel, that was located on the island of Hong Kong. We had to pass through the business district where the streets were crammed with thousands of people, venders, tourist and hawkers. After registering at the New World Hotel, we drop our luggage off and made a bee line for the streets. The business district was only two blocks from the hotel and the beginning of the shopping area. I could see the wheels turning in my wife's eyes when she saw the stores. There was nothing in this world you couldn't buy in Hong Kong, it was a shoppers' paradise. We window shopped until our tired bodies caught up with us and we couldn't take another step. We were going to be here for sixteen days, and decided the best course of action was to go back to the hotel and nap until dinner time. After dinner we walked to the harbor and took the Star Ferry to Kowloon, on the Chinese mainland, for more window shopping and little a night life.

The next morning we were on a bus bound for the Tiger Balm Gardens and its grottoes and pavilions exhibiting Chinese myths. The gardens were built by the makers of the Tiger Balm Salve that is touted as a cure for anything that ails you. I guess this would be along the lines of the snake oil that was sold on our western frontier in the 1800s. The statues and vases that were on exhibit were painted in shiny and gaudy colors, as were the dragons, snakes and the two headed monsters. The Buddha, were made of plaster and painted with high glossy gold paint, making them look very much like real gold. The flower and plants through out the gardens were beautifully trimmed and manicured to perfection. The brightly colored pagodas were positioned on the outer part of the garden where you could stand and see the steep side of the mountain where people were living in huts that were supported with bamboo poles. After lunch, our next stop was the Sung Dynasty Village, built more for the cultural aspects of China than the gaudy two headed monsters and dragons. This would be along the same pattern as the Tiger Balm Gardens, except here there was more entertainment, with tumblers, singers and dancers as well as restaurants serving traditional Chinese meals. One of the high lights of the Dynasty was the Chinese wedding ceremony that we watched from the beginning to the end. When the ritual was over we had our picture taken wearing the same robes that were used in the ceremony.

Aberdeen and the open market place were on the agenda for the next day. After breakfast we walked to the waterfront where we boarded the Star Ferry for a ride to Kowloon. From here we hopped a ride on a double decker bus that would take us to the market place and the Floating Village in Aberdeen. After arriving, we learned right away not to roam over ten feet from each other. The people in the market were standing shoulder to shoulder, it was just one big mass of humanity. As we were walking I told Jo to turn around and tell me what she sees. When she did she couldn't believe her eyes, there was a MacDonald's in the middle of this mass of humanity. We didn't eat there, but someone told us that they used kangaroo meat from Australia in their burgers. I don't know if this is true or not, I doubt that it was, but I'm just as happy that I didn't eat there. We also noticed there were a lot of camera shores here with every make known to mankind up for sale. If you were looking for an expensive camera at a bargain price, you were in the right place. We also learned right away that the owners of these shops are ready to bargain with you the moment you walk through the door. No matter what the price was, it's on sale for less. The first shop we walked into was only selling cashmere sweaters. The sweaters were "on sale" for fifteen dollars. The first thing the owner said was, "I give you good deal." After a few minutes of dickering over the price, Jo bought three sweaters to take home for Christmas presents for a total of thirty five dollars. Remember, these were 1981 US dollars. Bargains were everywhere and Jo made good use of them whenever she really wanted something. Later, we hired a sampan for a tour around the Aberdeen harbor to see the boat people. When you see this for the first time, you ask yourself, how can people live like this. Its' a community that consist of thousands of boats, sampans and junks of all sizes, where tens of thousands of people live their entire life. We saw a bamboo cage hanging on the side of a boat that housed live chickens. On another we saw a man sleeping in a hammock that was hanging on the side of the boat. In another, children were eating their lunch sitting on the back of their junk; with their feet dangling in water that wasn't the cleanest water I'd ever seen. These were typical of what we saw in the floating village. The big reason why these boat communities and the shacks we saw on the side of the mountain at the Tiger Balm Gardens, existed is the lack of land to build on. All of the flat areas have huge high rise apartments, stores, hotels and government buildings. In short, land is at a premium. We were told that an apartment sells for about one million HK dollars. After our tour of the harbor, we had the owner of the sampan leave us off at the Jumbo Floating Restaurant where we had lunch. Jo ordered a very appetizing looking green salad that she was enjoying, until she looked up and asked what the large looking marble was that was cut in half in her salad.. When she found out it was hard boiled quail egg, she never took another bite. I was sorry she didn't enjoy her salad, but I sure enjoyed my seafood salad, and I didn't care if a quail egg was in there or not. The restaurant itself was like a museum, it had a huge dining area decorated with all kinds of Chinese relics and paintings. The walkway and the entrance to restaurant had a display of carved teakwood items on tripods and shelves. After admiring this exhibit, we took a water taxi back to the landing in the middle of the market where we did a little more shopping before going back to the hotel. After dinner that evening, we went for a cable car ride to the top of Victoria Peak. It takes eight minutes to make the eighteen hundred foot rise to the top. The view from here is something you will never forget, particularly in the evening. The island of Hong Kong and the Kowloon Peninsula were all lit up like a Christmas tree, as was the Star Ferry and all the other water traffic that was moving. It was truly a magnificent sight and a great experience.

We had made arrangements for a two night stay in Bangkok, Thailand when we first arrived at the hotel. When we booked the trip, we wanted to be on the first plane to leave for Bangkok, so we wouldn't lose the better part of the day before we got there. Our alarm at the hotel was set for four in the morning because we were being picked up in front of the hotel at five o'clock, in order to make a six o'clock take off. When we landed in Bangkok we were met at the airport by our guide, and immediately started our mini vacation with a tour of the city and it was only nine o'clock in the morning. Our guide,

Specks, would be with us for the entire time we were here. She explained that she called herself Specks because of the glasses she wore and it was a lot easier for her guests to call her that, than to remember or pronounce her given name. When she gave us her name, I understood why. Bangkok, like Hong Kong, was like another world to us. The streets were crowded with people and shops of all kinds. The city itself is covered with brightly colored buildings decorated in yellows, reds, oranges and a lot of other combinations that are too many to describe. Besides the beauty of the city, the one thing you never forget is the "Toot-.Toots." These are three wheeled vehicles you see roaming all over the city. They look very much like an oversized golf cart, except they are driven by drivers whose pictures should be on wanted posters tacked on a post office wall because of their reckless driving. Our guide told us they were always having accidents and hitting pedestrians. While we were in the center of Bangkok, Speck stopped to let us do a little window shopping and get a great lunch at one of the fine restaurants. After lunch we took what little we had purchased to our hotel that we were seeing for the first time. We were staying at the President Hotel, called the Regent of Bangkok, which was located in the middle of the city.

After settling in at the hotel Specks took us for a visit to the Grand Palace in all its' splendor. Everything in and around the Palace is decorated in the bright colors of green, red, yellow and orange. As we walked around the grounds, we found it to be a fabulous Palace with all kinds of gilded spires and towers as well as statues of myths and goddesses. Thailand is a Buddhist country which explains why everywhere you go in Bangkok, Buddha is there, but none of them were as impressive as the Emerald Buddha that sits high on an altar in the Royal Chapel of the Grand Palace. When you enter the Chapel, you are immediately awed by what you see. The Buddha is carved out of a solid piece of emerald that's about three feet high and sits on a golden throne that is thirty four feet high, surrounded by statues and spires. Its' truly a magnificent sight to behold and you'll probably never see anything else like it again. After seeing the Emerald Buddha, we visited two more Temples. When we entered the Temple of the Golden Buddha, I found the Temple to be very small for the size of the Buddha. The Golden Buddha stood about fifteen feet high and made of five and half tons of pure gold, with a street value of about seven million 1981 HK$. I'm sure its' probable worth many times that amount today. But value aside, the religious aspects of the Buddha to the Thai people is priceless. When we visited the Reclining Buddha, I didn't see anything outstanding about it, except for its size. The Buddha was about one hundred and fifty feet long and covered with little pieces of gold flecks put there by the citizens of Bangkok when they come to pray. We only had time to see three different Buddha Temples, but from what I had seen, there isn't another that could compare to Emerald Buddha in the Royal Chapel. This was a very long day for us, we were up at four in the morning, hopped a plane to Bangkok and spent the rest of the day walking and riding on tours. I wasn't complaining, I was just tired and ready to hit the sack the minute we got to our hotel.

That evening we went to a Thai dinner show that consisted of portions of different Thai foods, served similar to the Chinese dim sum, which could be compared to a smorgasbord. After dinner we were treated to a classical Thai play. This was a drama where the dancers, dressed in the traditional and colorful costumes, would dance their parts instead of acting them out. It was a unique way of putting across the play, and I think I actually understood what was happening. I had mentioned to the guide when we first arrived that we wanted to see as much of Bangkok as we could in the two days we were to be here. I have to tell you she did a great job, because the first day was a perfect ten, "Toot-Toots" and all. We got another early start the next morning for a trip to the floating market. We took a ride with Specks to the Chao Payra River, where we boarded a water taxi that would take us to the canal that housed the floating markets. When we reached the canal, we got into another boat that was much smaller for a tour through the floating market. There were all kinds of long tail boats, most of them being paddled by women wearing big flat straw hats. These boats are very long, skinny and loaded to the gunnels with all kinds of fresh fruits, vegetables and hand made articles that were for sale. These canals are just like streets in a city except the people were paddling boats instead of driving cars. The scenery was very picturesque as you're passing vendors in boats doing a lot of chattering and hawking their wares. We even had the opportunity to see a small elephant lifting cargo out of a barge and loading it on the dock. Believe it or not we also a Buddha on a raft attached permanently to two sunken poles in the water. As I said earlier, Buddha was everywhere. The brochure we were given when we started said Bangkok was the Venice of the East. I've been to Venice, Italy and I can honestly say the only comparison between the two is, they both have water, but here it's a way of life.

The next day we started out for the Rose Garden Resort located outside of Bangkok, which is a must if you want to know about the Thai culture. We were entertained by the Thai Village Players, in what was a nonstop performance lasting about an hour and a half with tumblers, acrobats, sword fighting and of course lots of Thai dancing and singing. After the show we got to meet most of the participants in a court yard where we got to watch an exhibition with elephants that would put the P. T. Barnum Circus acts to shame.

On the way back to the hotel, we stopped off at a snake farm to watch two men milking cobra snakes for the venom. They would grab the cobra by the back of his neck and force it to open its jaws so the venom would flow out of the fangs into a petri dish. This venom would later be used to make anti-serum for humans who had been bitten by a cobra. You couldn't pay me enough money to do what they were doing. The hands and arms of the handlers were covered with big ugly scars from cobra bites. We only watched for a short time, but I saw something in that short time I would have never seen, if we hadn't stopped. Before we knew it, it was time to leave for the hotel to pick up our luggage and catch the last flight from Bangkok to Hong Kong. In the short time we were in Bangkok, we saw another culture that was very strange to us. I wish we could have stayed for a couple more days, because there was so much more to see. What we did see was only the tip of a pin, compared to what we could have seen. But, I wasn't disappointed at what I did see, only at what I didn't see.

We spent the next couple of days resting up in Hong Kong and taking in some more of the local sights. One of the things we did was to have High Tea at the Peninsula Hotel which was, at that time, one of the top ten hotels in the world. We were seated in a very fancy dining room where we were served two tiny sandwiches with no crust, along with some fancy pastries and cookies. The tea was poured into a beautiful colored tea cup, from a highly polished silver tea pot, by a white gloved server. This is a very formal British custom that I could never get accustomed to.

The following day found us on a hovercraft bound for the Portuguese territory of Macao. At that time there were only three ways to enter mainland China, by Hong Kong, Macao and Shanghai. After reaching Macao and going through customs to enter China we boarded a bus that looked very much like one of our old yellow school buses. The road we were on was just wide enough for the bus, which was really not a problem because we never had to pass another vehicle, only bicycles. As we were moving along, one of the passengers on the bus asked our guide if we could stop to take some pictures. She said, when we passed something interesting, she would stop the bus. The country side was full of interesting sights like a buffalo pulling a cart or men and women standing knee deep in a field of water planting or harvesting rice and the women using a big stones as a scrub board while washing cloths in a stream next to the bus. If this wasn't of interest to her, I can say for everyone on the bus, that it was to for them. I had already taken at least twenty-five photos through the window where I sat and through the driver's windshield of these, plus a few others. She wasn't the most cooperative bus guide I'd ever had, and she had a personality of zero to go with it. After a long ride we finally reached the village of Cuiheng, the birth place of Dr. Sun yet-Sen, known as the Father of the Republic, he was to China what George Washington would have been to us. From here we went to the village of Shigi where we had a lunch prepared Chinese style. Jo wasn't too crazy about Chinese food, she said half of it was raw and the other half is suspect. The truth is I didn't know what I was eating either, but I ate it anyway and it was very good. We had an interesting afternoon in Shigi looking for a souvenir to bring home, but there wasn't much to buy in this little village. But, I did see a small boy painting Chinese characters on pieces of orange parchment. His Mother was with him and she understood and spoke a little English. She asked if I would like to have her son put something on a piece of Parchment. I jumped at the asking, this was the kind of souvenir I was looking for. He put some strange characters in black ink on piece of orange parchment and handed it to me, while Jo took a snapshot of the boy handing it to me. Loosely translated it says, "The Big Man." I think he did that because I was so much taller then him. His Mother would not let him accept payment for it, so I gave him a full roll of life savors that I had in my pocket and when he saw them, his eyes lit up like two light bulbs. The parchment now hangs in wooden frame on a wall in my den. I couldn't have asked for a better souvenir.

We had four more days left of our vacation, two of which we would be using for our trip to Manila. We didn't realize it, but our room at the hotel in Hong Kong was getting smaller and smaller every day. There were bags and bags of souvenirs and other items piled all over our room. The only way we could get these things on our plane to bring home was to buy another piece of luggage. This had to be done as soon as we returned from Manila. This, along with the three bags we brought with us, would probably take half a day repacking them. In the morning we took a cab to the airport for the third and last time for a side trip. We were met at the Manila airport by our guide, Roberto, who was waiting on the tarmac to take us to our hotel. On the ride to our hotel, the Philippine Plaza, we discussed what we wanted to do while we were here. I 'm a big reader of World War II history, and wanted to see the island of Corregidor while I was here. Our guide said it was too late to do this today, but he would make all the arrangements for the next day. Today he had planned a tour of the city of Manila. Like Bangkok, there were some interesting vehicles running all over the city called a "Jeepney," which is half jeep and half jitney. Some of these kaleidoscopic colored vehicles were used as taxi cabs and others for personal use. Either way, they were driven by drivers who probably wouldn't be able to buy insurance in the United States, because of the way they drove these things. They ranked right up there with the "Toot-Toot" drivers from Bangkok. Manila is a city that was rebuilt after WWII, with many parks and statues of their past and recent heroes. Out of spite and hatred, the city was completely destroyed by the Japanese military when they were driven out of the city in 1945. It was hard to believe that Manila was ranked the second most destroyed city in the world during WWII. Except for the beautiful park there wasn't many things of interest to see on the tour with the exception of the dungeons in Fort Santiago, where political and military prisoners were tortured and executed by the Japanese and their past conquerors. Seeing Fort Santiago may have been interesting and informing, but it left me with a very sad and eerie feeling after being told what took place in WWII. That evening we had a typical Philippine dinner with lots of wine waiting for us at a night club that had been prearranged for us. After dinner we were treated to a dancing show with all the traditional Philippine dances. For the finale of the show, they did the Pole dance. This is a dance where four people hold onto two pairs of poles and bounce and click them while someone else is jumping in and out of the box the poles made. Unless you knew what you were doing, you could break an ankle at the drop of a pin. When they finished showing how it was done, they came into the audience and pulled two men up on the stage, me being one of them. They started bouncing and clicking the pole at a very slow pace, about one click every thirty seconds. At that speed both of us "volunteers" were able to do the dance without falling or making fools of ourselves. In the end, after a lot of clapping and laughing, it was a lot of fun.

We were on a pier the next morning at eight o'clock waiting to get aboard a Hovercraft that would take us on an hour long ride across the Manila Bay to the island of Corregidor, made famous for its heroic stand against the Japanese at the start of World War II. The island surrendered on May 6, 1942, after four weeks of brutal fighting and a last ditch stand. The soldiers who survived this brutal fighting were taken prisoner and later were part of the infamous Bataan death march. As you walk along the road that parallels the mile long barracks, you see nothing but the remains of what once were the buildings that housed the defenders of the island. None of the buildings were rebuilt or repaired to look as they did prior to the war. I did get the opportunity to walk through the Malinta Tunnel, but the laterals inside were blocked up by the bombing and never cleaned out. We were told that there were a lot of Japanese soldiers entombed in these laterals that had been used as a bomb shelter. The guide related every facet of the battles fought here, and we were very lucky in that there were only two other people besides us on the tour. It was like a one on one discussion all day long. As a result, he went into minute details of the hardships and carnage suffered by both the United States and the Japanese military. I had an eerie feeling walking around the demolished barracks and the destroyed gun emplacements. All that's left of the military theater, that was here prior to the war, is a shell of a building with no roof and partial sides. The last movie to be shown in the base theater in December, 1941 was "Gone With the Wind." I thought how appropriate the title of the movie was, since there wasn't much left of the place after the war. The only structure left standing prior to the war was the flag staff that is still operable today. There is a simple five sided monument honoring the place where marine paratroopers landed in

1945 and the men who were killed there. The island itself is of no military importance, it's as obsolete as the Magino Line in France and, the Fortress at Singapore, or the outmoded bow and arrows of the Western Indians. The last thing we did before leaving the island was to walk down to the waterfront where MacArthur and his family were evacuated to Mindanao by PT Boats, and later flown to Australia. The island was finally retaken four years later on February 16, 1945, and left exactly as it was on that day, as a memorial to what had happened there.

We got back to Manila, just in time to pick up our luggage and catch the last plane to Hong Kong. It seems like this happens every time we take a side trip. This entire trip was and still is the greatest vacation I've ever been on, and I can't think of another trip that could compare with it. I know I'm repeating myself when I say again, its' another world, but I can't think of any other words to describe it. Its' a curiosity, its' fascinating and its' very interesting. I would like to visit the Orient again someday, but I doubt that it will ever happen. Between the political climate, the civil unrest and world opinion, I wouldn't feel comfortable about doing it again. Who knows, I might even be disappointed if I did go back. Its' been twenty-nine years since that first trip in 1981 and that, was a long time ago. I know I would like to see a lot more but, I'll settle for the memory I have.

Can You Believe This – 1981

Star Ferry Kowloon

Floating Market Street Scene – H.K.

Aberdeen Market

Boat People

Street Scene H.K.

Pole Shacks

Street Scene – H.K.

9-2

Golden Buddha

Jumbo – Floating Restaurant – H.K.

1 US$ = 6 HK$

Floating Market - Bangkok

Chinese Wedding Attire

Chinese Wedding

Grand Palace – Bangkok

9-3

Working Elephant – Floating Garden

Cobra Snakes

Toot Toots – Bangkok

Milking Cobras for the Venom - Bangkok

Rose Garden – Bangkok

Thai Dancers

Street Scene – Shigi Village

Boy Painter

Dim Sum

Corregidor as it Was Left at End of WWII

Jeepney – Manila

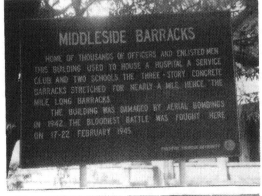

MIDDLESIDE BARRACKS

HOME OF THOUSANDS OF OFFICERS AND ENLISTED MEN
THIS BUILDING USED TO HOUSE A HOSPITAL A SERVICE
CLUB AND TWO SCHOOLS THE THREE-STORY CONCRETE
BARRACKS STRETCHED FOR NEARLY A MILE HENCE "THE
MILE LONG BARRACKS.
    THE BUILDING WAS DAMAGED BY AERIAL BOMBINGS
IN 1942. THE BLOODIEST BATTLE WAS FOUGHT HERE
ON 17-22 FEBRUARY 1945

Mac Arthur Escape Pier

Base theater

CHAPTER 10
CHICKS LEAVE THE COOP

Turning fifty in 1983 wasn't a pivotal year in my life it was just another year, but Jo insisted on having a big fiftieth birthday party for me. The entire family came, along with several friends of the family. I wasn't expecting a party of this size, but I felt honored when so many people came. The truth is I really enjoyed all of the attention and fuss that everyone made over me.

Except for my birthday party the only other excitement we had that year was a seven day trip to Brazil. We had joined a travel club recently that was offering these great vacations at a great rate. When the list of destinations had offered Brazil we thought it was a good choice for us. The only things I knew about Brazil were they grow a lot of coffee, eat a lot of bananas and the "Brazilian Bombshell" Carmen Miranda. But once you arrive, you realize that Rio is an amazing city with a different life style than we were used too. You go to bed at two or three o'clock in morning and get up at noon to take in the day sights. The night life and restaurants in Rio are outstanding. The concierge desk at the hotel made dinner arrangements at one of the restaurants for us and afterwards we would see a samba show at the the Oba Oba Club, which we were told, was the best show in Rio. We were caught of balance when he told us dinner was at ten o'clock and we would see the samba show at midnight. When he noticed the surprise look on our face, he said, "Its' carnival time in Rio." The show was everything he said it would be and the next night we went to see a different show at the Platform Club that was just as good as the one we saw night before. After seeing these shows, you get caught up in the music and you want to learn to dance the samba, because it's a fun dance. In addition to the shows, we gorged ourselves at restaurants that served a meal called Churrascaria. There is no menu, but a dozen waiters are walking around the tables carrying beef, chicken, sausages and fish on spits, along with trays of vegetable dishes and as long as you sit at the table they keep coming. We did this again at a different restaurant a few nights later and found out once is enough, twice is too much.

The main boulevard in Rio parallels all of the beaches. The three most popular and famous are the Copacabana, Ipanema and leblon. In the daytime it was fun just walking alone the main boulevard with all of their upscale stores on one side and the sandy beaches on the other. The most popular bathing suit, if you wanted to call them that, was the thong. Every girl on the beach was wearing them. I must admit they were a little skimpy, but I enjoyed the scenery. When we were not walking the boulevard, we were taking in other sights. We went to the top of Corcovado Mountain to see the statue of Christ the Redeemer. The next day it was a cable ride to the top of Sugar Loaf where we took in a beautiful view of Rio and the harbor below. Walking the boulevard and the beaches, as well as the sights we took in, were a lot of fun. But, the real fun was the night life in Rio at Carnival time.

I thought it was a long plane ride getting to Rio, but the ride back, seemed like an eternity. The coast of the United States was blanketed by a tremendous January snowstorm. We were turned away from landing in Baltimore, Philadelphia, New York and Boston. After flying around for a while, we were free to land at, of all places, Syracuse. We had to sit in the plane on the tarmac for two hours before we could get cleared by customs. Then we sat around in the terminal for two more yours before we were able to get back into the plane and on to New York. When we finally arrived, we were put on a bus and driven to Philadelphia. It was a real nightmare, but we'll always remember it because that's something you can't forget.

I never gave too much thought to my age, but as time passes it becomes harder and harder to accept the fact that your children were also getting older and would soon be making a life of their own. I didn't particularly like it, but I grudgingly accepted it, because I couldn't do anything about it. This was the year that it began to hit us as parents. Mike was married and living in North Jersey and Dan was on his own living in Philadelphia. Even though Joann was living at home, we knew it was just a matter of time before she also would be leaving. We talked about this on several occasions and came to the conclusion that our life wasn't over because they were leaving. As we looked around, we found that it was happening to families everywhere. Not only were my children leaving us, but this was true for Jo's sister Marie, who had five children, and our close friends Jim and Dorothy who also had five. Weddings were coming fast and furious in the eighties, when it wasn't one of ours it was one of Marie's, or one of Jim and Dorothy's. It seemed like the weddings were never going to end. By my count we have had eleven between us so far. The only one that hadn't tied the knot was Dan and he took the plunge in 1990.

In the Spring of 1984 we had the famous canoe trip that my sister-in-law Marie had planned. This was an example of the saying, "The best laid plans of mice and men." The plan was a five mile trip by canoe to a picnic area where Jo, my Mother-in-Law, and everyone else were setting up the picnic. At first I thought it was going to be a disaster, and in reality it may have been, but it also turned out to be one big laugh after another. Besides my canoe, watching six other canoes on a narrow stream was like six ice skaters who were on ice for the first time, they were all over the place. Nobody really had any experience, or knew what they were doing with a canoe, except, Michael, my nephew Bob and myself, but as fate would have it, the only one who tipped over that day, was me and my partner Marie. Putting Joann and her cousin Donna in the same boat was a comedy worth the price of admission. Donna did all the paddling, while Joann did all the complaining. If she wasn't fixing a broken fingernail, she was putting on sun screen while the canoe was bouncing off the banks of the stream because she wasn't paddling. To avoid colliding with her, Marie and I took a bath when our canoe flipped over. My nephew Bob just sat in his canoe, shaking his head while watching this fiasco. When we finally arrived at the picnic grounds everybody was laughing at Joann and Donna, while the two old timers, Marie and I took a ribbing for the bath. We were soaked to the skin and looked like survivors of a ship wreck. All in all we had a great time.

It didn't take very long, but what we both knew was finally here. We were used to the boys not being home, and now it's 1987 and Joann's turn, she would be getting married in October. I had never been involved with a bridal shower and I wasn't involved in the one for Joann. What I saw and heard that first hour before she came home to the surprise party was unbelievable. The house was full of women that were all talking at the same time and loud. There were so many conversations going on at the same time, I could not figure how anybody could understand or hear the next person. When I asked Jo how long this party lasted she said four or five hours after Joann comes home. I said this place is a mad house, I'm going to the driving range and hit a couple of buckets of golf balls, I'll be home for dinner

When the day came for the wedding I was all spruced up in my rental tux and ready for church. As I walked with her down the aisle on her wedding day, I felt this great feeling of pride, and at the same time a little sad at the thought of her leaving. I was told that I had a smile that stretch all the way to the back of my head as I walked her to the altar. I recall telling her, when was she was a little girl, that she couldn't get married until she was forty-five years old. But here I am, giving her hand away at twenty-three. As I walked back to the pew, after giving her away, I could feel a tear forming in my eye which made me feel a little uncomfortable in front of everyone who was at the wedding ceremony. But

I got over it and enjoyed the rest of the day. I might be a little prejudice, but I thought it was the greatest wedding that I had ever attended, and Joann was absolutely beautiful and in her wedding gown. When it time for the Father to dance with the bride another tear started forming. I tried hard to hide it, but when we started to dance, I couldn't, but I kept my composure and finished the dance. When the reception was over and she was leaving for our house to change, I said to Chris as they were getting in the limo, "I want her home by ten o'clock." He looked at me and laughed. The next day they left for St. Thomas and the honeymoon. It was kind of weird later to walk into a house that was quiet. I can no longer bark about the lights or the television being left on, the CD blasting in my ears or the doors left open in the winter and letting my heat go out the door.

At some time, every parent experiences the "Empty Nest Syndrome," when they finally realize and accept the fact that the chicks have flown the chicken coop for good. It takes a while, but eventually you begin to understand that their world is no longer your world. We were only sure of seeing the entire family together two or three times a year on the birthdays, but not all the major holidays, including Mothers Day. These were split between the families of the spouses because this was the proper thing to do. We were always seeing thirty-five to forty people sitting around our dining room table at Easter, Thanksgiving and Christmas. There may not be as many now, but we still have about twenty five or thirty, and we enjoy being with them. In the beginning we saw a lot of Joann, because she was the closest to home and she loves eating a dinner she didn't have to cook. I'm not saying she didn't cook, because she does, but its' not on her favorite list of things to do. She feels if Mom doesn't cook it, the only other choice is to sit down in a nice restaurant while someone else cooks it and then serves her. There are times when we don't see them for weeks at a time, but when they do come, it's always a joy to see them.

When I was in the Navy I spent about three and a half years of my time aboard one of two different ships and had the opportunity to visit several countries. The one thing I never did after leaving the Navy was to go on a cruise for a vacation. I never had the desire to go on one because I felt sailing from port to port was a waste of time. After listening to several people rave about the great food and the different show they saw every night while they were going from port to port, I thought it might be fun to try it once. The Regency Cruise Line had an interesting cruise scheduled for a trip to the western part of the Caribbean which included stops in Columbia, Aruba, Curacao and a trip through the locks of the Panama Canal into Gatun Lake where the ship would turn around and come back out on the same day. I had already been though the Canal once before while in the Navy, the only difference was the USS Ross went into the locks on the Pacific side and came out on the Atlantic side and we stayed overnight in Colon. The meals were everything they were touted to be and, the shows after dinner each night were excellent. The cruise wasn't as big a flop as I thought it might be. Once we got a taste of cruising it became our main vacation venue.

On November 25, 1990 we became grandparents for the first time when Joann delivered Alex. When the phone call came that the baby had arrived, we jumped into our car and made a made a bee line for the hospital. When I saw him for the first time he was four hours old and in Joann's arms. The first thing I did was kiss Joann, take a picture of Alex and put him in my arms after Joann handed him to me. Nothing could have made me feel better than holding him. He looked so frail and tiny in my arms that I handed him to his grandmother for fear of hurting him. For the next hour all we did was take pictures or talk about him. After leaving the hospital we stopped to buy a sign, which said "IT'S A GRANDSON," for our front where we proudly stuck it into the ground. We still have that sign in our attic as a souvenir of his birthday. Joann was very generous with him, she was forever bringing him for a visit, and to have us baby sit every chance she could get. Friday night was date night for her and her husband, it was something they had been doing ever since they were married. This meant we would have Alex to ourselves until they returned. We never refused to take him, but by the time he was three, he was here so often that he would hide when he heard them coming in because he didn't want to go home. We were worried that they might not want to leave him if he carried on like this, but they were never worried about it. When we asked Joann about this, she said, "I don't blame him for wanting to stay, if someone were buying something for me all the time and waiting on me hand and foot, I wouldn't want to go home either." Since Joann's old bedroom was the smallest I converted it into a room for him. We had all of what ever items belonging to him, put in that room. It was forever known as Alex's room. To this day whenever anyone stays here, its' still called Alex's room.

When Michael was born, I bought him a windup tractor, but with Alex I was more practical, he got a Jack In The Box. When wound up, it would play, "Pop Goes the Weasel," and when it hit the word "Pop" the top would jump open and "Jack" jumped about a foot high, making him laugh out loud. For the first few years all we did was play the song and he would watch and wait until Jack jumped out and we made a game out of it. This toy would give the two of us about five years worth of pleasure and smiles until he outgrew it. During that same time period he not only learned the "Pop" song, but was picking up the goofy songs I taught my children. Remember "Gut-a-roni" and "Wings of an Angel."

1992 was a very memorable year for me, not only was my second grandchild born, but I made the decision to retire. I reached the 55/20 rule the company had on the books concerning retirement, fifty-five years old and twenty year of service. In addition to that, the mortgage on my house was paid off, and since the children were on their own I couldn't think of another reason to keep on working. When I mentioned to Jo that I was thinking of retiring, she didn't like the idea at all. She gave me all kinds of reasons why I shouldn't She said I was too young to retire and I would be under her feet all the time. I wasn't expecting this reaction, but when I mentioned it to my children they were excited and thought it was a great idea. The only reservation they had was what I was going to do with myself. When word got out that I was leaving, the agents I was working with were stunned. One of them said I should wait until I was sixty-five or at least sixty-two to be eligible for Social Security. Another said I would be throwing away a big book of business. Another one said he wished he had the nerve to it, but couldn't afford to because he had a boy in college. When I mentioned to our friend Jim what I was going to do, he said if he had something to keep him busy, he would like to retire also. His only outside interest was his house at the shore and his business. My only answer to all of these reasons for staying were pretty much the same, "You have got to give me a better reason to stay then money." I felt as long as my children were gone, and the mortgage was paid, I didn't need a lot of money to live. When I became a neighborhood agent, I became a slave to the business. I never seemed to have any extra time for Jo or myself. I had seen other agents who stayed until after age sixty five but were gone by age seventy, or were stricken with some ailment or another, which kept them from doing anything. I didn't want this for me. In March I made it official, I gave notice that I was going to leave on or about September first. Now that it was official, I started to scale back my hours and the time spent in the office. I felt I could do this because I had a good staff to look after things while I wasn't in the office. Everything was going on schedule until I was informed by my doctor that I had a double hernia that had to be taken care of now. Since an operation was necessary I had to push my retirement date forward to December thirty-first. The operation was done in September and I was out on medical leave for two weeks. When I was sure everything was going ok, I kept my December date and retired officially on the last day of 1992. Allstate had been good to me in many ways, I didn't necessarily agree with some of the company's philosophy on business practices or the treatment of its agents. However, in the long haul it did provide me with a good living, benefits, profit sharing and, most of all, the opportunity to spend a lot more time with my children when they were younger. I can't think of anything I had missed during those years, because I had to go to work. I went to just about every recital, school play, JV football games and anything else that came down the pike. And as they say in a popular advertisement, "That's priceless, and you can't put a price tag on that."

Jo had said she didn't like the idea of me retiring because I would be in her hair all the time. Now after a year of retirement, Jo tells everyone that I was the busiest retired person she knew, because I was never at home. I was at the gym, playing golf, fishing, bowling, and if I wasn't doing any of these, I was planning something else. These were her words. I guess I wasn't as much under her feet as she thought I'd be. On occasion I would run into some of the agents I used to work with, and they would say retiring was the smartest thing I ever did, or I envy you. One of them asked me if I missed working, and I remember replying, "Yes on occasion, but the feeling only lasts for about ten seconds."

When we celebrated the New Year 1994, it felt strange to be sitting at home, instead of going to the office. The first year of retirement passed so fast I never realized how much freedom I had to choose where and when I could go somewhere. I was never much of a golfer, but I can now devote time to getting better. All I needed was some warm weather, a golf course, and time, of which there is plenty available now. I also joined a senior citizen bowling league which I still participate in today. I always enjoyed bass and pike fishing and now I've added fly fishing. There were lots of things Jo and I wanted to do and high on our list was to visit friends we hadn't seen in a long time. One of the first things we did was to plan a four week driving vacation through the South. We covered seven different states from New Jersey to Florida, with stopovers in every one. Before we left Audubon, we phoned all of the people we owed visits to and made arrangements to see them on the way. When we weren't visiting with old friends, we made overnight stays in cities like Savannah and Charleston, or stopping to see monuments and sites of the Civil War. When we started this driving odyssey I thought this might have been more than we bargained for. But time seemed to pass quickly, particularity when we stopped to visit with friends. If we planned to stay two days, we stayed three and they would want us to stay four. All of this driving may have been tiresome, but it was worth it, particularity visiting with old friends. Besides, we were in no hurry to go home, I was retired and we were enjoying ourselves.

Retirement is the reward you give yourself after years of raising a family, doing without or wishing you could do or have something special. Its' also the time to enjoy and spoil your grandchildren along with just sitting back and enjoy the life you have left, without any pressures.

Rio - 1984

Sugar Loaf

Canoe Trip – 1984

Joann 20 Years Old

Jim Halloween Party

10 Disneyland Me, Mouse, Jim 1987

35th. Class reunion

2

Children-Grandchildren- Nieces-Nephews-& Assorted Relatives - 1988

Regent Star – First Cruise 1988

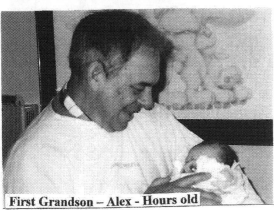

First Grandson – Alex - Hours old

New Orleans 1992

0-3

Giving Her Away

Dad & Mom

Dan – Mike   Joann Wedding

Paul-Barb-Me-Pat Joann Wedding

Dancing

Proud Father

CHAPTER 11
RETIREMENT & THE TRAVEL BUG

March of 1994 we went to Aruba with our friends Jim and Dorothy for a week of warm weather. It was a very lazy week for us, most of the time we were laying around on the beach and soaking up the sun. We rented a car for a week, but didn't use it very much except for a drive to the other side of the island and back just to see a natural bridge made by water and wind. The only other time we used it was to go into the town of Oranjestad for the girls so they could do some shopping. While they we walking their feet off, Jim and I were sitting in the shade drinking a gin and tonic and watching the world go by. This may not sound like an exciting vacation, but after the very cold winter we had, all we wanted to do was nothing. A week after we returned from Aruba I had a party for Jo. I bought her a Parakeet as a birthday present and she named it Ruba after the island of Aruba. Aruba is hard to say if you were to call him, so she shortened the name to Ruba. Everybody in the family enjoyed that bird for nine years before he died. After that she used his name as the password for her E-mail.

A vacation on an island is more relaxing, because you're in one place for a whole week and most islands are small enough to be explored in a few days. On a cruise ship you're always moving and while you're moving, its reading, dozing off on a beach chair at the pool, gabbing with new people, waiting or just laying around until the next stop. And if you're really energetic, you can go to the gym and work out. We were already bitten by the travel bug big time and once I retired, cruising would be my favorite way to travel.

We mentioned to our friends, Jim and Dorothy that we were looking into a cruise to the Greek islands and would they like to come along. They both said yes and when at the same time. They sure were easy to convince, this would be their first cruise. The cruise was for eleven days and we added three more days to take in the sights in Athens. We toured the Acropolis, the Temple of Zeus, and a full day trip to Delphi. In the evening we went to the Placka, an area just three blocks away from our hotel, where everything was happening. This area was full of narrow streets lined with restaurants and shops. We sat outside of a café the first night and had a three piece combo entertain us after dinner. The streets were all lit up and most of the shop fronts were open to the street. The last day was for the wives to do some shopping and later some more night life in Athens. The following morning we boarded the Stella Soloris and started our cruise. The first stop we made was Istanbul, Turkey where we took a tour of the city, visiting the Blue Mosque, the ancient Palace and the Grand Bazaar. Everything about the city is amazing, but the Bazaar was something else. It was over five hundred years and had over a thousand shops and stores that were covered from the street. It was like shopping in a gigantic cave. You could buy just about anything you wanted, we even saw a New York Giant football jersey for sale. After leaving the Bazaar we returned to our ship and headed for the city of Kusadasi and a side trip the ancient city Ephessis that was built in 135A.D. The ruins were in unbelievable condition considering its' age. You feel like you are there in its' hay day as you walked along the Arcadian way as did Cleopatra and Mark Anthony so many centuries ago. I wished we could stay a little longer to see the entire city, but the cruise ship waits for no one. From here we traveled to the islands of Rhodes, Santorini, Mykonos and Crete. Each island was a treat in itself, offering something different on each one. Crete was probably the most interesting because of the ancient city of Knossos, the site of the Minoan civilization that existed in the 15th. Century B.C. The frescos on the walls, particularly of the dolphins were in perfect condition. Its' hard to believe, since everything that is made today is built for obsolescence. When you buy certain things in today's market, after you pay for it you are asked if you want to buy an extended warranty on the product. It kind of makes you feel like the manufacturer doesn't any have faith in his product. From here we entered the Adriatic Ocean and set sail for Venice, Italy where we met our plane and flew home.

1996 started off with the greatest snowfall in the history of New Jersey weather up to that time. On January 8-9 we were hit by a snow storm that wouldn't quit. According to headlines on the front pages of the newspapers I had saved from the Philadelphia Inquirer and Camden Courier-Post, we had a total of 30.7 inches of snowfall that night and the next morning. This storm tied up New Jersey for the better part three days. Snow removal, loss of power, downed trees and icy roads were the culprits. But there was a silver lining, the sun came out and did its' job of melting the lions share of the snow.

When my grandson Alex was six we had a conversation about the pick up truck that I used to haul my boat with. He told me he was going to buy a truck like this when he was big. Whenever he came to visit, I would intentionally use the truck to run errands so that he could ride in it. I had given him an old fishing cap to wear and he would instantly run for it and grab one for me so that we could use the truck. He thought you had to have a hat on in order to use the truck. I told him when he was old enough to drive, and he graduated from high school, I'd give him this truck. Every so often he would remind me so I wouldn't forget. I once told him, when I make a promise, I keep it. I started to take Mike fishing when he was pretty much the same age, and I thought it might be the right time to let Alex try. I remember the first time I took him fishing and both of us were wearing our fishing hats. When I asked him if he would like to go and he gave a resounding yes. The bass club I belonged to had a small pond in back of the club house that was full of sunfish, bass and a few small catfish. I thought this might be a good place for him to start. He didn't like the idea of putting a worm on the hook, but he liked the idea of fishing. I helped him make to his first cast, handed him the rod and told him to look at the bobber. When it goes under the water, lift the pole up. As luck would have it he got a hit on the first cast and pulled in his very first fish, a bluegill about six inches long. It took me about five minutes to untangle the mess he made of the line, because it became one big birds' next of line, but that goes along with the teaching. He was so pleased with himself when he held that fish up in the air with the hook still in its mouth. After I took the hook out of the fish's mouth, he refused to touch it because the fish was flopping all over the ground. I finally got him to hold it while I took a picture of him and the fish. That picture is in a frame hanging on the wall in his bedroom today.

In September we went on a cruise with Jim, and Dorothy to Sicily. We left Philadelphia in the evening and landed in Marseilles, France the next morning. After boarding the cruise ship we had enough time before sailing to take a three hour tour of Marseilles. After a bus tour of the city we sailed for Italy and our first stop, Naples. When we arrived in Naples, we opted for a day trip to Sorrento and a harrowing and twisting ride on the narrow Amalfi Highway. The road is built on the side of a cliff overlooking the ocean, which looked to be a half mile down when looking out of a bus window, moving at fifty miles per hour on a narrow two lane highway. To make it even scarier, I don't remember seeing any guard rails, but I must admit the view was breath taking. Sorrento is a beautiful city to visit, but if I ever get to see it again, I think I'll wear a parachute if I take the bus.

After boarding our ship we set out for our next destination, Venice. We skirted the island of Sicily to enter the Adriatic Ocean on our way to Venice. Jo and I had been here before, when we took our unforgettable bus trip around Italy. This time it was more relaxing and we got the chance to see what we missed the first time. All Jim talked about was the Gondola ride he wanted to take, so that was the first thing we did. After the tour of the canals we took a water taxi to St. Marks Square for lunch. After that, Jim and I found an outdoor table, ordered a beer and watched the people go by. We had no desire to go shopping with the girls. After a second beer, they showed up loaded down with bags just in time to go back to the cruise ship for our stop in Sicily.

After docking in Messina, we boarded a bus for a trip to the town Taramina, which is located in the mountains. There wasn't much to do here, except it was a picturesque little village with a lot of shops and stands selling souvenirs. The village itself wasn't much, but the country side was like a scene out of the "Godfather." There were rocky hills, narrow roads and olive trees everywhere. We passed by a walled in house that I swear looked just like the one in the movie scene where Michael's first wife was killed with a car bomb that was met for him. But what really made this trip memorable was the ride back to the ship. It took an hour to get to Taramina from the ship, but over eight hours to get back, with six of those hours in the stand still position. While we were in Taramina, there was a very heavy rain storm in the mountains that caused massive mud slides that backed up traffic everywhere. One of these slides went through a mountain village that was on the opposite side of the road we were on. We could see cars and houses covered with mud and later finding out several people from the area lost their lives. Mother Nature really stuck her tongue out at the people in that village. We watched men with snow plows pushing mud from the highway as if it were snow. All told there were over twenty bus loads of passengers going back to the ship from all over the area. We were detoured down to the coastal highway, and crawled along all the way back to the ship. Usually if you miss your ship, you are left behind and on your own to catch a ride to the next port. In this case it was after midnight and there were over four hundred tired, hungry and irritated people stranded. When we got back to the dock, the ship was still there waiting for us. The passengers who were on the ship were lined up along the ship's railings cheering and clapping when we arrived. We felt like heroes returning from a war. When we finally boarded the ship, we were ushered into the dining area where hot food was waiting for us. What I had witnessed that day will never be forgotten.

After leaving Sicily we headed for the port of Livorno, the stop that would take us to the city of Florence. Lined up on the dock, where we tied to, were buses that were waiting to take us to Florence or the other destinations you might have signed up for. Jo and I had been here once before for two whole days, and now we have a few hours to see it again. Florence is more than a city, its' one big giant museum where every building you enter is a treasure of history. Its' the birthplace of the Poet Dante, and the Medici families, who inspired the birth of the Renaissance that produced the great artists, sculptors, and architects of the time. The Uffizi Museum and the Pitti Place are full with paintings of the Masters. The Galleria building houses the sculpture of David along with hundreds of other pieces of art. The Ponte Vecchio Bridge, which looks more like a building than a bridge, is not what it once was, its' now occupied by goldsmiths, jewelers, and art dealers. This bridge is the only one that was not destroyed during WWII. This was our second time here, but no matter how many times you visit Florence, there's never enough time to see and enjoy it all.

The year 2000, "The New Millennium," is a once in a thousand lifetime's event. Think about that, there are only a few billion people in the world that will be able to say, "They lived it that year." A few billion sounds like a lot but, it's a drop in the bucket when you consider it will be another one thousand years before that can happen again. In the year 2100 there won't be many people over a hundred years old that can say they witnessed the coming in of the New Millennium. But if there were, who would care, it'll be another nine hundred years before it comes around again.

This year also produced the greatest fishing experience that Mike and I had ever had. We were fishing in the Northern Canadian Province of Manatoba, where we caught and landed in one day eleven master northern pike (pike over forty-one inches long) plus an additional seventeen trophy pike (pike over thirty-six inches). It was an unbelievable experience and that neither one of us will ever forget. Our guide on this trip was amazed at what we had done. About a month later I received a card, with a note attached that describes my relationship with my son Michael. After reading it my thought went back to my Uncle Angelo. In August, 2001 I went to my fiftieth high school class reunion, and the ranks of the living were shrinking fast. A lot of the friends I had made were now gone and I felt very sad when their names were announced. Its funny how you take life for granted, even though these people are no longer with us, I still remember the good times, the kiss, the dates, the dances, the hikes, the lake, the swimming, and everything else that I had done with them. I felt that this was probably the best reunion thus far that I had attended, and I've been to all of them except one. I say this because everyone was more relaxed, older and not as judgmental as when we were younger. I think we were all happy just to be walking on this side of the grass. We had a party one night and played golf the next morning. Then we visited with one another in the afternoon and evening at different places. Late in the morning of the next day it was a picnic until about three o'clock when everyone left to get ready for the banquet that night. It was a short three days, but it felt like a long time while I visited with all of my close friends. A few of us had breakfast together the next morning before we said our good bys. I left with a smile, as I'm sure most of the rest did the same.

In October we were on a cruise with our friends Jim and Dorothy again, this time to the Black Sea. Even though we had already visited some of the ports of call, the duplications of the stops were well worth it in order to see the Ukraine. We picked up our cruise ship in Istanbul, Turkey and set sail into the Black Sea and our first stop Varna, Bulgaria. We were only there for a few hours and didn't get to see much of the city except for a quick tour of an old Russian Orthodox Cathedral. Outside in the court yard there were at least fifteen tables displaying beautiful hand knitted sweaters and needle work of doilies, napkins, tablecloths, shawls and bed covers that were for sale. We were told these women would spend all winter long, plus the normal work they had to do, making these things to sell whenever they found the opportunity. It was almost sinful for how little these women were asking for their work. The few cruise ships that did stop here were their main source for sales, and they were only good for four months of the year. Our next port of call was Yalta, which for Jim and I was one the main reason for the cruise. Being a history buff on WWII and coming to Yalta where the Conference with Stalin, Roosevelt and Churchill were held was a big deal for me. Livadja Palace, the Site for the conference, was setup in the original room exactly as it was in 1945. The walls surrounding the master table, where they were seated, was covered with blown up pictures and photograph that were taken at the time of the meeting. The Palace was beautiful with lots of memorabilia pertaining to the meeting and the history of the Palace itself. Yalta and the Palace, as it looks today, with its manicured lawns, equally spaced shrubs, flowers, and everything else spit and polished. It is not what it looked in 1945 when the "Big Three Meeting" was held. The city had been under siege for months by the Germans when they invaded it, and later by the Russians when they took it back. From here we sailed to the city of Odessa, in the Ukraine, where we were treated to a ballet at the Odessa Opera House. It was a beautiful building, oval in shape, with very high ceilings decorated with golden frescos and surrounded by walls that held works of art and sculptures. It was like looking at the past in all its glory. Having never been to a real ballet before, I was truly impressed by the theme of the ballet, the Russian Revolution, that was set to music and dancing. From here we were taken on a tour of the city and its parks. Our guide told of the devastation inflicted here during the war years, when it was occupied by the German Army and later fought over by the Russian Army. Most of the buildings had to be repaired or rebuilt, after the war, but somehow the Opera House survived with very little damage. Like Yalta it was hard to believe a war ever existed there with its beautiful parks and buildings. After leaving Odessa we went back to Istanbul where we would stay for another day. This gave the girls another visit to the Grand Bazaar for more shopping. The next day we were on our way to Athens, and after that to Venice for the trip home. I really enjoyed this cruise, but the stops in Yalta and Odessa were the true highlights for me.

September 11, 2001 will also be a date I shall never forget. I was sitting down to some breakfast, when the television program I was watching was interrupted with the news flash that an airliner had hit one of the twin towers in New York City. A few minutes later another news flash showed a second plane hitting the second tower. This whole thing was developing right before my eyes. It was as though I was watching a movie with some unbelievable special effects. Terrorist had driven two airliners into the New York Twin Towers, killing over three thousand people, and a little while later, a third airliner was hi-jacked and crashed into to the Pentagon in Washington DC killing one hundred and sixty more people. When a fourth airliner crashed in a field outside of Pittsburgh, with over fifty more people lost, I wondered when was it going to stop. To quote what President Roosevelt said in 1941, when Japan attacked Pearl Harbor to start the second World War, "This is a day that will live in Infamy," and I believe this will also. This senseless killing dragged us into a conflict in the Middle East that still goes on today with more senseless killings and destruction by a people who have no feeling or conscience of what they are doing. As I see it now, it will be a long time before we ever get together and shake hands.

In March we booked a trip to South America with the Jim and Dorothy for an October sailing. Because of the terrorist attack in September we were a little nervous about leaving the country. I had never been nervous about flying before, but this was a Different matter. After a lot of discussion with ourselves and our Travel Agent, we decided to go. We boarded our plane in Philadelphia and flew to San Diego, California where we were to meet the cruise ship. After going through all of the security checks we felt much better about the whole trip once we landed. Before boarding the cruise ship, we went through a port authority building for even more security checks. But, once we boarded our ship, all we could think or talk about was where we were going. We would visiting Costa Rica, Ecuador, Peru and Chile, stopping at eight different ports. After leaving San Diego we were at sea for two days before we reached our first stop in Puntarenas, Costa Rica. Here we boarded a bus for a trip into the interior of Costa Rica on our way to the town of Heredia for a tour of a coffee plantation. We were met there by a cast of professional actors who escorted us around the plantation coffee field to show us how the coffee is grown. We got to see how the beans were picked and where they were taken after. They made a joke out of the commercial showing Juan Valdez picking the coffee beans and putting them one by one into a sack on the back of a donkey. From here we were taken to a theater to show us how to recognize and taste a good cup of coffee. After the tour we went to Valle del Sol for a very delicious barbecue. On our way back to the ship we stopped at a rest stop in a small village where we were entertained by a make shift band.

We weren't here for a long time, but this band had us in stitches while we were there. They were playing a version of Yankee Doodle that I had never heard before. I doubt that any two of these "musicians" were playing in the same key or tune at the same time. As much as we laughed, we absolutely enjoyed it. They may not have been on the same page, but they were entertaining. Everyone on the bus clapped and we all left a big tip before leaving.

After leaving Costa Rica we set sail for Guayaquil, Ecuador, but first we had to cross the Equator. We crossed it at night and the next morning there was a big ceremony for all Polliwogs, (people crossing the Equator for the first time). It's a ritual that I'm unable to describe, for the lack of words to describe it, but I can tell you this, you will kiss King Neptune's belly, bathe in Davy Jones coffin and go through many other rituals before it's over. Finally, to make it official, you must kiss a big dead slimy fish on the lips, which means you have become a lifetime member of the Royal Order of the Shellbacks. You are no longer a Polliwog, but a Shellback for life with all of its privileges, whatever they may be.

The next morning found us tied up to the pier in Guayaquil, Ecuador called the "Pearl of the Pacific." Whenever you go to a large city for the first time, there is always something out of the ordinary that stands out in the memory of your visit. Guayaquil is a city of over 300,000 people and rich in history with old architecture and many museums. It also has a very unusual cemetery called "Civdad Blanca" (White City) where no one is buried under ground. Because of the high water table, the permanent residence of the cemetery are entombed above ground. Everyone has a huge headstone in various shapes and sizes. Some look like miniature skyscrapers, while others look like giant spears pointing to the sky. The very wealthy inhabitants have mausoleums with giant oversized angels looking down on them. My memory tells me there wasn't a small headstone in sight. I can only come to the conclusion that they all wanted a grand send off to the great beyond. I know that New Orleans has a cemetery like this, but there is no comparison to what I saw in Guayaquil. You probably think I'm a morbid person because I have this memory but, you must admit, it was unusual.

Our next stop was Lima, Peru where we tied up to a pier around seven in the morning. By eight o'clock we were on a bus bound for the National Anthropology and Archeology Museum. Our guide was feeding us all kinds of information pertaining to the Inca culture as we moved along in the museum. Here were collections of mummies and tapestries, as well as other artifacts of the Inca culture. Going through here was like taking a trip into the past. From here we were taken to the ruined city of Pachacamac, built around the year 700AD, where we explored the remains of a temple built to honor the gods of the

Sun and Moon. Considering the age of the temple and walls of the buildings they were in great shape, the only thing missing were the roofs. Walking around and through these ruins was like walking in footsteps of the past. The next stop was the highlight of our bus tour. We were guest at the famous Hacienda Dos Valle Ranch located at the foothills of the Andes Mountains. Unless I'm mistaken, we were told that this ranch is one of only two places in the world that raise and train horses to prance. While the lunch was being prepared, we were entertained by a fascinating exhibition of Andrean horsemanship. The horses were ridden by Gaucho clad riders who could do more on the back of a horse than any rider I've ever seen. After the show we had an outdoor lunch of beef, chicken and various vegetables that were cooked in an underground pit. The pit had red coals on the bottom covered with large green leaves. Meat was added and then alternate layers of leaves between the chicken and each vegetable that was to be cooked. The cooking started well before we arrived, because it takes several hours to prepare and cook a meal like this. It was served in clay bowls reminiscent of original Inca dinning ware along with several different Andean wines. This was supposed to be the way the Incas' dined many centuries ago. It was more like a feast than a lunch, after which we headed back to the ship for "dinner" at seven. I don't remember anyone of us eating a big meal that night, but we did celebrate Jim's birthday with a cake, candles and singing happy birthday.

Arica, Chile, only twelve miles outside the border of Peru, was our next stop. Instead of a bus tour into the interior of Chile, we decided to spend, what little time we would have with an hour tour of the city, and taking in its' sites. Arica is called the "City of Eternal Springs" due to the mild weather it has year around. It's also a very popular tourist city because of it's sandy beaches, its' shops and places to see. One of the most unusual sights is the San Marcos Church built in 1876 of iron and steel with wooden doors. It replaced the original one that was washed away by a tidal Wave in 1869. The city also has an interesting history. Arica at one time was actually part of Peru. It was the primary port for the entire nation of Bolivia and the city of Tacna, Peru. Because of some political differences, in 1879 Bolivia and Peru declared war on Chile, called the War of the Pacific. Chile won the war and through a treaty it occupied Tacna. In 1929 the three countries finally came to an agreement, giving Chile the city of Arica, Peru was given Tacna and Bolivia was allowed to use Arica as the only port of entry to their country.

Coquimbo/La Serena was our last port of call in Chile, before debarking in Valparaiso We decided that all we wanted to due here was walk around the city for a couple of hours, doing a little shopping and then head back to the ship and start packing for our plane ride home. Chile is over three thousand miles long but less than two hundred wide. The drive to Santiago would take about two hours, so we had plenty of time to make a couple

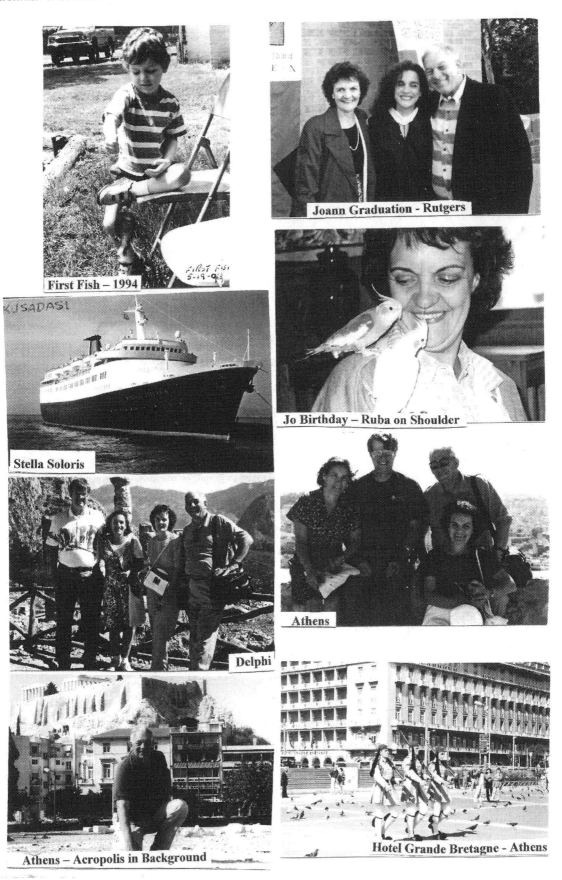

First Fish – 1994

Joann Graduation - Rutgers

KUSADASI

Stella Soloris

Jo Birthday – Ruba on Shoulder

Athens

Delphi

Athens – Acropolis in Background

Hotel Grande Bretagne - Athens

Temple of Zeus

Zeus Gardens – Athens

Istanbul Harbor

Blue Mosque – Istanbul

Celsos Library – Turkey

Arcadian Way – Ephessos

Mykonos

Castle Built by Knights of Ste. Johns
During Crusades - Rhodes

121

Monday, January 8, 1996

It's Two Feet And Counting As Record Storm Hits Region

Tuesday, January 9, 1996

50 Cents

Region Struggles to Dig Out From Record 30.7-Inch Snow

Four die; further snowfall expected

By Anthony R. Wood

As the biggest blizzard in the area's history ended, life in the region was virtually suspended yesterday.

And likely to stay that way for a while.

45th. Reunion

Alex & His Truck - 1992

Gondola Ride Venice

122

11-4

SATURDAY, JANUARY 1, 2000

Hello, 2000!

Calm reigns around the world as new year begins

50 inch Northern Pike

48 ½ inch Northern Pike

Odessa, Ukraine

**Portrait Hanging in Livadija Palace
Where War Ending Conference was Held**

Ste. Marks' Square – Venice

June 24, 2000

Knee Lake RESORT
MANITOBA · CANADA
Experience of a Lifetime
1-800-563-7151

I learned a few things this
week fishing with the
Biviano's. Some things about
fishing but most importantly
about people. I not only
learned but saw it each
day on the water and that
was a father and son
can be the best of friends.

Dan Meyer

Class Reunion – 2001

Andean Horsemen

Inca Ruins – Peru

Andean Dancers

SanJose Band – Costra Rica

Crossing Equator

Jim Birthday

Guayaquil, Ecuador   2001

Montana or Bust By-Pass Trip

Yellowstone River

Dan

Steak Dinner

BY-PASS FISHING TRIP

Ready to Launch

Nice rainbow

Mike

Lunch Break

CHAPTER 12
THE BIG SCARE

On August 28, 2002 my Mother passed away at age 92. Three days later on August 31, Michael and his bride Lynn were married. I had seen Mom at the hospital in Syracuse just the week before, and knew that the end was near. Even though she was gone I tried to enjoy myself at the celebration of Michael's wedding, but she was on my mind all day. The next day Jo and I left for Norwich to attend the funeral the following Monday. The newly weds delayed their honeymoon in order to attend the funeral and the following day they left for St. Thomas. My Father passed away just a few days before Michaels' first marriage. Nineteen years later his Grandmother also passed away, leaving him with these two unhappy memories.

I celebrated my 70th birthday in 2003 with my entire family plus several friends. I felt honored that so many people came to celebrate the party with me. To make sure the occasion would be remembered, seven days later we had twenty-five inches of snow fall. This was the largest accumulation of snow since the thirty inches had fallen in 1996. Jo had given me a snow blower for Christmas and this storm gave me the opportunity to play with this new toy for the first time. Even in a snow storm, you can find a cloud with a silver lining, if you look for it.

December 2003 turned out to be a bad years' end for me, I lost my very close friend Jim on December 8.th He and his wife Dorothy were our constant traveling companions whenever we went on vacation. In the early years we would get away for an occasional weekend in the Poconos. This was about all we could afford, but as the years went by we began to take week long vacations and later started cruising. We had met in 1968 when Jim and his two sons were signing up for cub scouts. Neither of us knew then that this would be the beginning of a life long friendship that would last for thirty-five years. He was always telling some of the dumbest jokes I ever heard. The one thing that always stood out about him was the way he laughed at his own jokes. Sometimes he would actually double over with laughter, but as corny and as dumb as they were, I miss him telling them.

Four day later on December 12 my mother-in-law also passed away. When Jo and I were married, she and I were constantly at odds with each other over everything. She would want one thing for Jo and I would want something else. As the years passed the two of us started to realize that we both loved Jo, and we had our lives to lead without interference from the outside. We also found out that we had many things in common, one of which was a hands and knees interest in gardening, and flowers in general. I loved the way she cooked Italian food, especially the broccoli she would make for the holidays. The fresh crab sauce she made for spaghetti wasn't that bad either. I remember one time when Jo and I were in Ventnor for the weekend she bought a dozen crabs and made a pot of crab sauce. Jo was not particularly fond of crab sauce, so Mom and I sat down and ate the entire pot of crabs. When we finished, there was sauce everywhere, including the wall next to the table and the floor. Sucking the sauce out of the crab legs was half of the fun in eating them, but Jo thought we were a couple of slobs because of the mess we left. I also want to tell you that my mother-law had some expressions that make your mouth drop and the Pope blush. If that were one of us when we were young, we would probably have our mouths cleaned out with soap. But that was her and how she really was. I miss her too.

Even though the holidays were sad, we celebrated Christmas with the families in Ventnor. Jo stayed the rest of the weekend with her sister, who was having a difficult time coping with her mother's passing. I had things that had to be done at home and errands to run, so I left. When I got home, I made myself a shopping list and took off for the supermarket and the malls. As I was walking around the market I started to feel a little uncomfortable. My head started spinning, I was sweating heavily and I could feel my eyes closing. I remember reaching for the bread rack to steady myself so I wouldn't fall. I don't remember the fall, but I do remember looking up and seeing a woman asking me what was wrong. I don't think I answered her because my eyes went shut again. The next thing I remember was kind of funny. As I opened my eyes I saw what I thought to be a two man SWAT team coming towards me, and later realized they were paramedics that came because of the call the store manager made to 911. They were dressed in blue with their pants inside of high top shoes and wearing vests that made them look like they were members of the SWAT team I had seen on television. By this time, I was pretty much awake and aware of what was happening. The paramedics were taking my blood pressure and asking me all sorts of questions, and then telling me they were going to take me to a hospital. I said I wasn't going to go to any hospital, they insisted and when I again said no, one of them handed me a piece of form to sign. They told me this was a waver form, when I asked what waver, this is the answer I got. "If you refuse to go, that was my right, the waver was to absolve them of any blame if I drove my car home and on the way I killed myself, or anyone else, they were not responsible, I was." It looked like I didn't have much of a choice, so I went. I was taken to the emergency room at Cooper Hospital in Camden where all kinds of people were checking me out. If they weren't checking my blood pressure, they were taking my blood, or putting an IV in my arm, while someone else was hooking me up for a cardiogram. After the testing, I was told I did not have a heart attack, but they wanted me to stay over night to continue to monitor me, to see what caused the blackout. No one in my family knew I was in the hospital because I didn't have a phone number for where Jo was. But one of the nurses was able to get a hold of my daughter Joann, and she managed to get in touch with her mother. When I was finally taken to a room, they again hooked me up to my monitors. Joann was the first to see me, when she saw all the tubes and wires hanging, I could tell she was overcome by what she saw. When Jo finally arrived, Danny along with Joann and Earl were already there and Mike was on his way. Once he arrived I now had the entire clan there and started to feel better about things. The next morning the cardiologist came in and told me I definitely did not have a heart attack. He also said I could go home if I promised to call his office Monday and make an appointment for a stress test. I said I would, and on Monday they scheduled me for a test on January 7. A stress test is a medical procedure that takes about three to four hours to perform. Briefly, what they do first is to take your blood pressure, then inject cardiolite, a nuclear substance, into your arm through an intravenous to see how well your blood is flowing. After sitting a while to let this substance go into your blood stream, you are taken to another room where you lay under a MRI type of scanner that takes pictures of your heart. When that's over, you sit around for a while and then you're taken into another room where a technician wires you up to a monitor. Once this is completed, you stand on a treadmill and hold on for dear life. It starts out slowly, but gradually increases its' speed, while the monitor records what's happening in the heart. Once it reaches its' limit, it gradually decreases its speed until it finally stops. When the treadmill stopped, I was gasping for air because of the fast pace I was keeping up with. If I didn't have a heart attack before stepping onto that treadmill, I felt sure I was going to have one when I got off, panting as hard as I was. When you're finished, you go home and wait for the phone call that gives you the results. When it came, I was again told that I did not have a heart attack, but would have to be catheterized to make the final decision. In this process they inject an iodine based dye into an artery in the groin to allow it to go through the blood stream to the heart. I was pretty much aware all through this procedure, but I got a little nervous when an hour went by and I'm still on the table. I asked the doctor what the hold up was and he said he couldn't talk now because he was kind of busy. At that moment I knew I was in trouble. When they were finished I was told I had four blockages, three of which had to be by-passed. I'm told that if the blockage is sixty percent or less a by-pass isn't done. I had three that would require surgery, two of which were over ninety percent. I asked if there was any other way to handle the problem, and was told that I could be monitored until it became absolutely necessary to have this done, which means it would probably be critical. If I chose to do it now, it would be on an elective surgery basis, which means easier to survive. Deep down I knew I really didn't have much of a choice so I said, "What the hell, lets do it." When I went back to my room to change into my own clothes the nurse said, "Mr. Biviano, I heard you chose to do the operation. You just bought yourself another ten years."

On January 28, 2004, one day before my seventy-first birthday, I was going to have surgery on my heart. Up to this point, I only knew a few people who had any kind of surgery on their heart. One of them was my mother, who at the age of eighty-two had a valve replacement and one by-pass. She lived to age ninety-two. My granddaughter Mattie had heart surgery at the age on nine. I know a couple of others, but not as personal as the two above. I remember Jo standing next to me holding my hand as I lay on a gurney waiting to go. The anesthetist came in and said, "I'm going to give you something to relax you." From that moment on I remember absolutely nothing until I woke up many hours later sitting in a wheel chair and gagging on this thing they put in my mouth so I wouldn't choke on my tongue. Jo was still standing next to me holding the same hand. I couldn't talk, only gag and make sign language, mostly pointing to my mouth. Later, a nurse finally came in to remove it. I was put into a room with another heart patient, where I was to remain for the next eight days.

I had three different room mates during my stay, but the last one was the one I shall never forget. He was a man who had no idea of how serious it was to have a heart problem. He was brought into my room on the fourth evening, in pain, with a pacemaker that was not working properly. The nurses were trying real hard to calm him down, but he was not cooperating. When he finally realized they were trying to help, he laid back and let them do their job. A doctor came in to have a talk with him, and assured him that everyone was doing all they could, and he was to relax and stay calm. Right after this episode, Jo came in for a visit and introductions were made. He got out of bed, pulled a chair up next to his bed, leaned back on the chair with the two front legs off the floor and put his feet up onto the frame of his bed. Both Jo and I held our breath and said,

"What are you doing, do you realize what would happen if you were to fall backwards?" All he could say was "I'm not going to fall." However, he did lower the chair, probably thinking we were right. We talked for a while until visiting hours were over and Jo left. I laid in bed thinking about a lot of different things, when for some unknown reason I started to think about the kids when they were young. I laugh out laud about something my son Dan had done, and he walked over to the bed and asked if I was alright. I told him what happened and we started to tell each other our life's story until the wee hours of the morning. When we finished he said I should put the stories of my kids in a book so that everyone could enjoy them as much as he did. I told him I wasn't interested in a book, all I wanted to do was get out of here.

I was looking forward to going home on the sixth day, but a complication caused me to stay two days longer then was intended. That night I felt so sorry for myself that I started to cry, and just laid there wallowing in my own self pity. After a while I started to realize how truly lucky I was, this was not an emergency and I didn't have a heart attack. When Jo came the next morning I felt better about myself and my situation, but never mentioned what happen that night. The following morning the doctor came in and said I could go home. All I could do for the next six weeks was rest and take it easy. I walked a lot, first around the inside of the house, and then short walks outside and finally long walks around the neighbor-hood. I did everything I was told. In March I started my rehab, three times a week for twelve weeks. While I was there my old roommate from the hospital came in unexpectedly. We shook hands, passed amenities, and then he asked if I had done anything about writing the book. I told him I hadn't given it much thought and was only thinking about my rehab and getting back to normal. That was the last time I ever saw him. After completing the rehab and taking another stress test I was released. I still take a stress test once year and visit with the cardiologist twice a year.

The first thing I wanted to do after rehab was to go on my annual fishing trip with Dan and Mike. I had asked the doctor back in March if this would be possible and he said, no reason I couldn't, but to wait until July. When I asked him in July, he said yes to August. I called to make the arrangements, and on August 8, Mike, Dan and I were on our way to Montana. On August 6, seven months after my by-pass, Mike, Dan and I took off for Boseman, Montana. We had two guides and two boats so we could spend the same amount of time with each other by alternating a different boat each day. This was the first time I had ever been out West to fish. This trip was a long ways from the early years when we would go to the St. Lawrence by car and stay in a rented cabin. The trip was a total success for me because the three of us were together for the first time in many years. We had a lot of laughs and good times together. We even caught a lot of fish.

We drifted the entire length of the Yellowstone River, over sixty miles in seven days, from Gardiner to Livingston. This was the first time the three of us had been on a fishing trip together since the summer Dan was working in a bait shop on the St. Lawrence River. A week after I returned from Montana Jo, her sister and Jim's wife Dorothy left for a vacation, leaving me home alone. It had been eight months since my bi-pass surgery, and things were finally looking up. The live well on my boat needed to be fixed, and since I was home alone, this would give me something to do.

While drilling holes for the new bolts, the drill hit the netting on top of the well and pulled the drill over my hand, severing my ring finger from the top to the first knuckle. The entire incident only took about half a second, and when I looked at my hand I knew I was in big trouble. No one was home to help and I was bleeding pretty heavy and in no shape to drive a car. I wrapped my whole hand in a towel, ran outside and rang every door bell I could find. Finally one of my neighbors came to the door, I explained what happened she ran for her keys, put me into her car and took me to my family doctor, luckily was only three blocks away. He took one look and got in touch with the hospital telling them I was on my way and to have a hand surgeon ready. A police car took me to the same hospital that did the by-pass. While this was going on he had his nurse call my daughter Joann, telling her I was on my way to the emergency ward at Cooper Hospital. While my finger was being attended to, Earl and Joann come in and the first thing Joann said was, "When until Mom sees this, she's going to have a fit and the first thing she's going to say is, Richard, I can't leave you alone for a minute." Joann hit the nail on the head, that's exactly what my wife said. Its' been seven months since my by-pass and now I'm looking at four more weeks of rehab for my hand. There are many times in our lives when we'll run into the unexpected, then we look up at the sky and say, "Why me God?" That's what I said.

Later, after I explained what happened, we talked about where the girls went and what they did on their vacation. I mentioned to her how good it felt to be fishing with the boys again and how nice it would be to go on a vacation as a family again. She agreed with me, and was thinking about the same thing. We thought that a cruise would be perfect, that way we could spend time with them on the ship and take tours together when we hit port. In September, when the clan came to celebrate our anniversary, we told them about the cruise, they cheered and said it was a great idea. When we told them we were going to the Caribbean, the cheers became even louder. We discussed the dates that were available and the next day we booked the trip for March, 2005. This would be the first time we were to be together again as a family on vacation since our trip to Man and His World, in Montréal, Canada in 1974.

The year 2004 ended with a Tsunami Wave that hit the southeastern part of Asia so Hard it left a death toll exceeding two hundred thousand people. It was one of the greatest natural disasters in the history of mankind.

MOM 2000 (passed on Aug. 2002)   Mike/Lynn Wedding Aug. 2002   Bridal Party

Mom & Dad with Mike

The Bride

Shuttle Plane to God's River

God's River Guide – 2002

Monday, February 17, 2003

12-2

SLAMMED

Severe storm may leave more than 2 feet of

Car Before

Car After

Jo's Mom My Birthday

USS New Jersey – Alex

Dan – Joann – Mike

Ring Finger – 2004

CHAPTER 13
THE FAMILY CRUISES TOGETHER

In January we celebrated not only my birthday, but also the first anniversary of my by-pass surgery and it felt great. It was hard to believe that it had been twelve months since the operation. The days may have passed slowly, but the year went by fast. Six weeks later we celebrated Jo's birthday, but the topic of conversation was the cruise. Up to this point no one had ever been on a cruise except for Michael's wife Lynn. All they talked about was what they were packing and what they were going to do on the trip. A week later we were boarding our plane for San Juan, Puerto Rico where we would pick up our cruise ship. The cruise included six island stops at St. Thomas, St. Maarten, Antigua, St. Lucia, Barbados and finally San Juan. They were all beautiful islands, and we toured everyone of them. There were way too many stories to tell because every day was different, and it would take forever to tell them. They were acting like little kids going to Disneyland for the first time. It was one big laugh after another, every day it was something different. One night Danny talked all of us into going to ship's Casino to play blackjack. We found an empty blackjack table and took over all the seats. A family that cruises together gambles together. The pit boss was enjoying us as much as we were enjoying ourselves. He said he had never had an entire family sitting at his tables before. We may have been a little rowdy but we were having a good time. At dinner the next night the pit boss sent a bottle champagne and a bottle of wine with the complements of him and the ship's captain.

There was a bingo game every day which started with a jackpot of five hundred dollars that would grow every day until someone won. Some of us played on occasion, but by the last day at sea no one had won as yet and there was three thousand dollars in the jackpot plus a cruise for two. Everyone on board the ship showed up in the auditorium to play including my gang. Joann wasn't a bingo player, but on this day she decided to play. The jackpot was to be played with a complete blackout. There are twenty-four numbers and a free spot on the bingo card and every number has to have been called in order to win. The game started and there were eight numbers had been called when up jumps Joann and yells, "BINGO, I WON, I WON, I NEVER WIN ANYTHING, I WON." Everyone in the auditorium was looking at her kind of funny. I leaned over and said, "Joann there weren't enough numbers called for you to win." What she had was a normal four numbers and free spot bingo. By this time everyone was laughing and the bingo caller said, "She must have had a special with twenty-five free spaces." It took ten minutes for the laughing players to quiet down and continue the game. Joann was really embarrassed and all she could say was, "Darn I thought I won the money and the trip." She became an instant celebrity when everyone realized the mistake and were kidding for the rest of the cruise, but she was a good sport about the whole think. We imitated her all night long, and the more we did, the harder we laughed. The next morning we docked at the pier in San Juan and waited to debark from the ship when our turn came. After leaving the cruise ship we had four hours to kill before our flight would take us home. We found a restaurant in San Juan where we had lunch and one last big laugh before boarding our plane. We all went home with a great tan and no burns because we bathed in sun screen. The only one who had a problem was Lynn, who had gotten a nasty rash and a reaction from touching cashew shell when we were on the island of St Lucia.

For me this was truly a memorable cruise for all of the good times and laughs we had together as a family. I'm sure everyone will always remember this cruise with fond memories.

The cruise to the Caribbean may have been over, but it was still the topic of conversation for a long time. We were all caught up in reminiscing with each other about the happy and funny things that happened on the cruise. Mike and I were also caught up in it, but our focus was on the up and coming fly fishing trip on the Madison River in Montana. We had been fishing together since 1974, thirty-one consecutive years without a miss. In addition to the great fishing, we had seen many interesting things over the years. The old Indian markings, a fantastic aerial view of the Tetons as we landed in Jackson Hole and the scenery and wild life of the Canadian North Country, to name a few. But the one experience we had this day ranks very high on the list. We witnessed something that very few people, except for the ones living in the West, would ever get the opportunity to see. Montana is the fifth largest state in United States, but very few people in comparison to its size. One thing it does have, besides great trout fishing, is cattle and land. On our way to the Big Hole River our guide mentioned that we would be a little late getting to the river because of a cattle drive coming our way. Sure enough when we went around the next hill, facing us was a heard of cattle coming straight for the truck. I don't know how many head of cattle there were, but my guess would be a couple of hundred. Because of all the private property, the land is fenced off to everyone. As a result the cattle have the right of way on the road when they are being moved from one grazing area to another. When I saw them coming, I stuck my head and video camera out of the door window and started taking a video of the whole scene. There were men, women and young boys on horseback driving these cattle, and it looked just like something out of a John Wayne western. The only difference between these cowboys and the western movie cowboys was these cowboys didn't carry a six shooter in a holster strapped to their leg. I can also tell you that the cattle left a disgusting looking trail of waste on the road surface after passing us. We may have lost some of our fishing time that day, but it was worth the price of admission to be in the middle of that cattle drive. On our way back, after fishing the better part of the day, we passed through Virginia City. This little town was one of the gold rush settlements of the 1860's. It isn't much of a town now, but back then it was the home to a several thousand miners who were panning and digging for gold. As we rode through town, our guide was giving us a fast history lesson of what was once a wide open lawless town. The miners would break their backs all day long panning and digging for the gold, and on Saturday nights they would spend a lot of their gold dust in one of the many gambling halls or brothels in town. After about fifteen years the gold pretty much panned out and the miners move on to new gold fields, leaving this as a ghost town. We could see pieces of the old mining equipment, railroad cars and huge piles of stones and rocks where the miners had been panning and digging. What we saw that day was all that was left of the town to remind you of the miners' existence. The fishing was great, as always, but this one day and the cattle drive were the highlights of this year's trip.

In July I attended my fifty-fifth class reunion. Time, age and illness was hurting our Class attendance, there were only about thirty-five of us, plus their spouses, that were able to attend. As the reunions pass, I see less and less of my classmates attending for many reasons. Some are not able to travel because of illness, while others have passed away. When they call the names of the departed at the banquet, I feel sad, not to be able to see them one more time. Even though the numbers had dwindled over the years, I still manage to have a good time with those who came. It might be playing golf in the morning with foursomes made up of classmates followed by a two hour lunch afterwards. It might be a get together in the evenings at someone home, who still lives in Norwich, and the next morning going back for a barbecue. Most of the time there's a picnic in the morning followed by our class banquet in the evening. It doesn't make any difference what we're doing, because we're with our old friends one more time. I know the numbers will be even smaller at our 60th reunion, but I still look forward to that 2011 get together and meeting again with the one's who are still here.

After returning from my reunion, Michael and Lynn informed us we were going to be Grandparents in March and its going to be twins. They showed us photos of the ultrasound that was taken, but they didn't want to know if they were girls or boys. As a result they were known during the pregnancy as baby "A" and baby "B." I had never seen an ultrasound photo of an unborn infant before, but when I saw this one for the first time I didn't see much of anything. But later as they were taking more photos, I could see the forming of different parts of the body, like a foot or a spine. The more times I was able to see them, the bigger they got. I couldn't wait for the time to come when I could see them fully grown for the first time. But while we all were waiting, we had a cruise to take. In four weeks we would be on our way to Seattle, Washington to pick up the cruise ship to Alaska. We would be gone for seven days, stopping at the cities of Juneau, Skagway and Hounah in Alaska and Victoria, B.C. in Canada. It's a good thing we checked the weather before we left, because it was in the high 80's in Philadelphia, but in Alaska it was in the 60's. Remember its August and very hot here, but not there. On the family cruise to the Caribbean we were putting on shorts and sunscreen, but in Alaska we were putting on hooded sweaters and jackets. Our first stop was the city of Juneau where we took a side trip to the Mendenhall Glacier. After seeing this we walked a trail to Steep Creek to see where the salmon were spawning. The guide pointed to the high grass along the creek where it had been matted down, and covered with salmon carcass that were left there by feeding bears. We didn't see any bear here, but nobody really wanted to. After this, it was back to Juneau for lunch at the Red Dog Saloon, then a shopping break for the girls before leaving for the ship. At our next stop, Skagway, we joined a jeep convoy that was going into the Alaskan interior. There were five jeeps in our convoy plus one more on each end that were driven by our guides. Each jeep has four riders, you do your own driving, but you are always in touch with the guides. We got to see everything from beautiful scenery to wild life. We stopped several times to see distant glaciers, bear along the sides of the road and an eagle haven where injured eagles were nursed back to health so they could again fend for themselves in the wild. After four hours of sight-seeing, we headed back to Skagway and a visit to the Red Onion Saloon. The saloon was built in 1890 during the big gold rush, and according to the brochure, this was the first exclusive bordello in Skagway. We were waited on and served by young women dressed in the costumes of the day with a flashy garter on her leg. From here it was back to the ship and a stop in the village of Hounah, where we went through an old cannery that dated back to the 1920s. There was very little automation back then, everything was done by hand, but it was interesting to see how they packed and sealed the salmon in the cans. The town is about fifty years behind the times, but it did have one good restaurant, The Office Bar that served fresh Dungeness crabs. I don't remember how many crabs the eight of us ordered, but it was a lot. When we finished, our table looked like a huge Crab shell dump that was piled high with empty crab shells and dirty, messy napkins I'm glad we didn't have to clean the mess. From we went back to the ship and set sail for our next stop Victoria, Canada. From here it was back to the ship We didn't take any tours here we just walked around the water front where all of the street lamps were decorated with baskets full of brightly colored flowers hanging from the street lamps arms. We spent a lot of time in front of the beautiful and majestic Empress Hotel that's located on the waterfront. This was the most popular area of the city because of the free entertainment, the view, the trendy shops and the great restaurants. From here it was back to Seattle and the airplane ride to Philadelphia. The cruise may have been a little tiring because of all the tours and walking we did, but everyone said they had a good time, in spite of the cold weather, but they wanted to go back to the Caribbean where it nice and warm. I want to admit that the Caribbean was a lot morn fun. The skies were blue, the sun was out and the weather was hot all the time, but Alaska was something to see.

Christmas brought the family together for the traditional holiday dinner. This was when we found out that the twins were not going to term. The due date had been in March, but because of a problem that Lynn was having, they would have to be taken from her within the next few days. After Christmas everyone was waiting for the phone call from Michael telling us when. A week later I got a call from Mike telling us a date had been set. When I asked him when, he answered "In two hours." All I could say was, "Mom and I are on our way." By the time we got there, the twins had already made their entrance into our world. On January 5, 2007 at 2:19 PM. Baby "A" (Julia) arrived weighing four pounds and two ounces. Baby "B" (Bridget) followed at 2:20 PM weighing three pounds and nine ounces. Mother and the twins were doing fine. Looking at these tiny little things in an incubator made a tear roll down my cheek. I was amazed at how tiny they were, I had never seen a baby that small. I thought Mike was tiny when he was born weighing five pounds ten ounces, but he dwarfed them in comparison. A couple of days later I was given Bridget to hold for the first time, she was so light it was hard to tell if I even had hold of her. On January 13 Lynn was discharge to go home with Julia, but Bridget had to stay in the hospital for five more days because she needed to gain a few more ounces. We didn't get to see her during these days, but when she came home we were there to greet her. When Alex and Mattie, our other two grandchildren, were born they only lived a few minutes from us, so we got to seem almost daily. But Mike and Lynn were living ninety miles away and it was a long ride to see them on a daily basis. But we did make it a point to drive back and forth twice a week

Normally you have children in your younger years of marriage. You are also socializing with younger couples who are having or already raising a family. Since both of you are in the same boat, its only natural that you compare notes about raising children. In Michael's case he was forty-nine years old when the twins entered his organized world. In over twenty prior years of marriage, he never had to think about children, he just enjoyed his job, his easy life and the vacations he was taking. He didn't have the slightest clue about raising a child, let alone two of them at the same time. He couldn't understand why they cried so often, or why they didn't want to sleep at night. I was on the phone with him one time when he was telling me that I didn't realize how hard it was for him to get up at six o'clock every morning, after getting only a few hours of sleep because of a one A.M. feeding. My answer was, "Who do you think was doing this when you were born?" What he didn't realize was that everyone goes through this in the early years of marriage, when they're raising a family. I told him I didn't know much more than he did, I couldn't put a diaper on right, but I learned fast. It was a little easier for me, because my first experience as a father involved one baby and not two. I think it was also easier raising children when we're younger, because the older you are, the more set in your ways you are. I remember saying "I loved my children, but I could have loved them more if they were housebroken and could talk." This, of course, was not true but only a fleeting hope on my part. His wife, on the other hand, came from a large family with eight brothers and sisters along with a lot of nieces and nephews. He may have been a little slow in the beginning, but he learned fast. In July, we were on our annual fishing trip, and as always, we caught lots of fish, had a lot of laughs and a great time. Instead of talking about a hundred different topics, most of the conversation was about the twins and how he missed them. This was coming from a guy who six months earlier said to me they cried too much and didn't sleep enough. He's also the guy that said, "He couldn't wait until our fishing trip, to get some peace and quiet." Now he tells me how much he misses them. I think he's finally beginning to get what it's all about. Jo and I spent all of what was left of 2007 by going back and forth to see the twins. When we were not going to see them, they were coming to see us. It was an absolute pleasure watching them grow from two tiny babies into gorgeous little girls. We had been watching them crawl, standing up by holding on to something and finally walking. The first time we were to see them in our house, after they started to walk, we decided to child proof the kitchen, living room and rec. room before they came. I took great pains in making and using buffers, gates, and latches to keep them away from anything that might hurt them or break. When I was finished the inside of the house, it looked like a fort without cannons. When the day was over and they left to go home, we gave a big sigh of relief. But in spite of the time we spent picking up after them, wiping finger and hand prints off the TV screen, taking all the buffers down and putting the rooms back in order, we still were looking forward to having them again. I guess you could say, we were gluttons for punishment. On Mother's Day weekend we received the news that we were going to be grandparents again in November. They again didn't want to know whether it was going to be a boy or a girl. It didn't matter to us what it was, but it sure was a shock when we got the news. Dan and his wife were having problems which lead to a separation and finally a divorce. He was taking it very hard, and to make matters worse, he had lost his job. He seemed to have lost his self esteem and had a lot of crazy thoughts going around in his head. He was living alone in an empty house and we had to convince him to that he needed help right away. It took a long time and a lot of care before he was himself again. Good paying jobs were hard to find because of the financial crash that took over the entire country back in the October. The bank collapses caused many big companies to layoff workers by the thousands, and small businesses to fail. It was a case of, for every job that was available, twenty people were applying for it. While he was staying with us, he spent all of his time on our computer answering job ads, going to interviews, and sending resumes on the Internet. While all this was going on, we received the telephone call we had been waiting for. On November 3, 2008, Mike called to say we were grandparents again of a baby boy names Nickolas, then added we can now be assured that the family name will be carried on. The next morning I was holding him for the first time. He was a chunky little guy that weighed six lbs. and eleven ounces at birth. That was just a few ounces less than the twins weighed together when they were born. We celebrated Christmas at our house that year and Nickolas took center stage and was the main topic of conversation all day long. A week later, on January 3, we celebrated the twins second birthday and on the twenty-Ninth my birthday. We did a lot of celebrating in November, December and January.

Finally, in January Dan was offered and accepted a good job with a company located in Wyoming. He flew to Wyoming the following week, for a person to person interview with the new employer. While he was there, he found an apartment then came home for all his belongings. He said it was everything he was looking for and he would be starting in two weeks. It was a long way from all his problems and he was getting a new start in life. He also mentioned that there was some good trout fishing there. Two days later, on January 28, one day before my seventy-sixth birthday we loaded his car with everything he could carry, said our good bys and he was gone. We hear from him once in a while, mostly by E-mail, but he managed to come home for two days at Christmas time.

When my grandson Alex was a little boy, he said when he grew up he wanted a truck of his own. I told him when he got a drivers' license and he graduated from high school, I would give him my truck. He never forgot that promise, because he mentioned it every now and then. On June 6, 2008, I handed him the keys to the truck and told him it was his to keep. It had been a long wait for him and when I finally handed him the keys, I thought he was going to bust, he was so happy. I was very proud of the way he turned out, he was a good student in school, always polite, good manners, and I can't think of him ever getting into any serious trouble. Today he is attending collage and working towards a degree in Engineering.

Five days before Christmas, December 20, 2009 we were hit with the first of four big snow storms. This one dropped over twenty inches of snow on us in one night. On February 6, I didn't think the snow would ever stop falling, but when it did the next day we had 27 inches on the grown. No sooner had we shoveled our way out of this storm, four days later on February 10, we had another 16 inches of snow that we really didn't need, followed by another eight inches six days later, giving us a total of over seventy inches of falling snow in less then seven weeks. This was not a great way to start 2010.

Start of the Family Cruise

The Girls - St. Thomas

Informal Dinner

BINGO !

St. Lucia

Blackjack Table

Dan – Mike
St. Maarten

Rowdy Ending

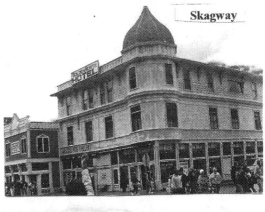

55ᵀʰ. Class Reunion

Alaska '06

Skagway

Hoonah

Welcome to Alaska

Highway 7 – Alaska

Jeep Caravan

Breakfast Before going Shore

Red Dog Saloon

Going to After Dinner Show

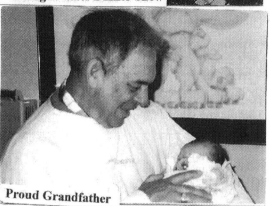

Proud Grandfather

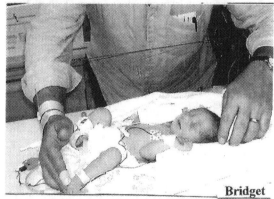

Bridget

Finally Alex Gets his Truck

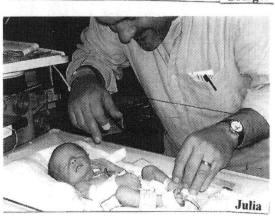

Julia

Everyone Home

Twins – 2 Weeks Old

Pool 7 Months

Bundled up 9 Months

Redfish Caught in Louisiana Bayou - 2008

Nickolas One Week Old

BROKEN: 65.5 INCHES

BLIZZARDS RULE

Stores, offices take a snow day in region

By EILEEN SMITH
Courier-Post Staff

Many retailers, banks and

Storm sets new mark; more snow may follow

By LAVINIA DeCASTRO
Courier-Post Staff

CHAPTER 14
SUMMATION & OBSERVATION

I began to write this journal in October of 2005 and I thought I had finished in 2007, but I thought wrong. Several months after the book was printed I picked it up and read it again from beginning to end, when I was finished, I was amazed at how much I had left out. Reading it again brought back more memories that I had completely forgotten about the first time plus I now have the addition of three more grandchildren to enjoy. Its' been a long time since 1990 when I became a grandfather for the first time, and 1993 for the second and what I thought would be the last time. To my surprise and happiness, fourteen years later, a set of twin girls, Bridget and Julia, and a year later another grandson, Nickolas, came into our life. I really enjoyed being a father, but being called Grandpop is something entirely different and very special. I've heard other grandparents say they love their grandchildren but they're always happy when they go home. I never really felt that way because I always wanted to see them, even though they made a lot of noise and a mess while they were around.

As I look back to my past, I began to think about my father and my relationship with him. I tried very hard to understand why he was like he was. He had a lot to offer us, but he chose not to. He may not have finished high school, but he was a pretty smart man. He did wall papering at night as a second job, and figured out square footage in his head for the amount of wall paper needed to do the room. He filed his own income taxes and helped his sisters and brothers do theirs. He knew how to build things and modernize a house, in short, he was a Jack of all trades. He was very close to his brothers and sisters but, for some unknown reason he could not seem to connect with his own family. I'm not trying to assassinate his memory, or looking for any sympathy, I just want you to understand how it was. Many years later, the only reason for his behavior that I can come up with, is he was bitter at the way life turned out for him. He was a man who was a product of his time, where everyone in the family worked for the good of all the family. I think he felt he could have done better for himself and his family if he had been given the chance. In short, he was angry with the hand he was dealt. I've discussed this with my sister Pat, and she agrees. I think this along with the difficult depression years didn't help matters any either. By the time my younger brother and sister came along, things were better financially in the household. I left home when I was eighteen and never really came back except for an occasional visit, but it was what it was, and I couldn't do a thing about it. He passed away in his sleep at the age of seventy-four. I feel sorry for him not having what I now have, the closeness of my wife and children, and I hope he found peace with himself.

My mother was just the opposite of my father, as I saw him. She had a hard time making new friends, because she was not an outgoing person, but she always had time or me. She was a strong woman and in fairly good health until her middle eighties, when she started to lose her eye sight and later after having heart surgery. She was four months short of ninety-three when she passed away on August 28, 2002. I miss her very much and I still think her about a lot. I hope I inherited her longevity gene, because I want to see how all of my grandchildren turn out.

I like to think my children's childhood was fun for them, because they had a Mother and Father who participated in their lives. By the same token, I knew they thought I was a royal pain in the rear when it came to the rules of the house, like homework, curfew, clean rooms etc. But now I know they have to deal with these same rules with their children and I just look at them and smile. By the time children reach the age of thirteen or fourteen they seem to think they are wiser then their parents, who are definitely not with it. However, when they reach their early twenties, they're amazed at how much we learned during those same few years when they thought they knew it all. In some ways they made growing up very difficult for themselves by not following a few very simple rules concerning curfew, dinnertime, and chores. We tried to stress that being a good citizen, doing the right thing, being polite, and earning your own way, was the right way to live. Its' unfortunate that a lot of today's youngsters can not accept accountability for their behavior and manor, but I like to think mine did. I stressed the value of a family relationship as they were growing up. A family is supposed to stick together in good and bad time, with everyone pulling in the same direction, and giving moral support when its' needed. I wanted them to remember that friends are great to have and they should have lots of them, and treasure them, I know I did. But the truth is when push comes to shove your family is all you have. My parents, as a team didn't show the outward signs of love and affection that I now thought they should have. My Mother did most of the time, but my Father did not. I only know that we were there for ours. The time you spend with them as they are growing up, is like money in the stock market, it comes back to you like as a dividend. I know the three of them are as close as peas in a pod today, because they're always on the phone either talking to Jo and I or each other. And when they get together for a family function, everyone really enjoys each others company

Life is precious and priceless, and all the money in the world can't buy it. You may be able to extend it a little, but that's all. You can be a world leader or the pillar of society, but if you ignore your family, you have nothing. I was foolish one day in the supermarket when I kept refusing to go to the hospital, not because I might kill myself or someone else, but because I owed it to my family to be there to take care of them. If, the paramedics had not convinced me to go, I may not have been here to tell this story. Being macho only works in the movies, its part of the script and in real life it isn't like that. The only thing that really counts is how you lived your life. You can be rich or poor, it really doesn't matter, what counts is family. Like the end of a family or the end of an era, what else do we have but memories, and these should be, and I stress should be, passed onto the next generation. After putting this story on paper, I realized I didn't do so bad for a boy with low esteem. In a few more months I'll be celebrating my fifty-third year of married life, and that in itself is a moral victory by today's standards. The closeness I didn't have when I was growing up, I found when I married my wife. Her Mother was the kind of person that demanded family togetherness. As the children came along to us, and her sister Marie, it was a constant party every month of the year. When it wasn't a birthday it was a holiday like Christmas or Thanksgiving. At first I thought too much was made of the family get together, but later I could see the bond that held this family together. My nieces and nephews as well as my children are now taking over what their grandmother started and their own parents continued. I'm sure when the time comes, their children will also carry it on, because that's the way they were brought up. My Mother-in-Law is gone now, but I thank her for showing me how important the family unity really was. If I had Aladdin's Lamp, I doubt that I would want to change much of anything in my adult life because there's nothing much to change. The good times, and there were many, I'll always remember. The bad times I've pushed to the back of my mind and I try hard to ignore them, but I know their there. It would be difficult to forget the bad times anyway, because they did happen and will always be there. Thinking back to some of them made me realize and appreciate how good I really had it. I feel I made the best out of my life with the hand I was dealt and have no real regrets. I relied heavily on my photo albums to write this journal, because it was easy to relive it. A photo is very much like a diary, except you relive the time or moment with pictures instead of words. Someone once said,

"A picture is worth a thousand words," and I believe that. I was constantly referring to these albums, and had the feeling that I was writing a series of short stories. But again, that's also what your past is, a series of short stories, with every day and every event being a little bit different. Not only did the pictures bring back the memories, but the memories brought back more memories. Playing Chutes and Ladders, Checkers, Monopoly and later Chess as well as the card games Old Maid, Go Fish and Rummy with the kids will never be forgotten. I remember hearing a lot of tall tales about how big the fish was that the boys caught or that got away. I think the fish grew an inch every time they told the story. I still remember taking Joann to see Snow White when she was five years old. Writing about my own childhood was very difficult because all I had were flashbacks or specific events like the war years. It was a shame that there were very few pictures taken during those early years. I remember seeing a box camera that my parents had, but it must have been broken because I never saw them use it. I was lucky to have two cousins, Bob and Christine, who were able to supply me with some old snapshots of their parents, who were my Father and Mothers' sister and brothers. I may have had to jog my memory for those early years, but after that, it was my seventeen albums of pictures that came alive. There was no way I could recount everything in the albums, and believe me there were many more, if I did, this journal would be as thick as Webster's Dictionary. The only vice I had, if you want to call it a vice, was fishing. Ever since my uncle gave me that old fly rod, I have never been able to put one down since. The time I spent with Mike and Dan fishing was a gift I gave myself. I wish I was able to attach a copy of the 8mm video that I had given to Jo for her birthday in 1985. It was packed with stories and occasions that I am unable to put into words. But, I hope you get as much enjoyment reading this journal as I did in writing it. This is where my story stops, December, 2009

After the kids left home I had three empty bedrooms, so I made one into a den for myself that I think of as my "I remember when room." There are photographs, paintings, and memorabilia of all kinds hanging on the walls and sitting on book cases and shelves. I had a hard time trying to find a suitable title for this book. While I was reading the final manuscript I realized that most of the good times I had with my children growing up, were always associated with the drink "Kool-Aid." I didn't notice at the time, but the years spent living on Graisbury Avenue were magical. I say this because every time we have a family get together today, some event always pops up. It might be the rice pudding Jo makes, and someone invariably asks, "Is it the Upper Volta receipt with the raisons and whipped cream?" But no matter what it was, Kool-Aid seemed to be with us everywhere, from the cub scout outings to day trips, the drive in theater or Man and his World in Canada, it was always there. I wasn't a big fan of this drink back then, but looking back on those years and what my own youth was like, I think I can now say that the Kool-Aid ain't so bad after all. So I leave you now, with a pitcher full of ice cubes and lime Kool-Aid, along with day old cupcakes and a peanut butter and jelly sandwich.

The end of the story,

but there's more to be told.

The end of the memories,

but I know there' more.

153